'Short, droll and highly readable, *Grown Ups* is
a slice of life that rings painfully true'

'I absolutely loved this book'

'I would strongly recommend to anyone who is
looking for a holiday read with a punch'

'The pages just flew by'

'This is a fantastically crafted novel'

'Sensitive, emotional, and littered with the kind
of tongue in cheek humour that I love'

'Very clever, wonderfully translated'

'The Scandinavian setting was the icing on
the cake, it was perfect escapism!'

'A complex, layered story'

'Every word [was] perfectly judged'

'Full of simmering tension'

'A potent little gem of a novel… Outstanding!'

'A really poignant read with humour and
drama scattered amongst the pages'

'An excellent examination of family dynamics… I loved this'

'Perfectly formed'

MARIE AUBERT made her debut in 2016 with the short story collection *Can I Come Home With You*, published to great acclaim in Norway. *Grown Ups* is her first novel; it won the Young People's Critics' Prize, was nominated for the Booksellers' Prize in Norway and is being published in 15 countries.

ROSIE HEDGER was born in Scotland. Her translation of Gine Cornelia Pedersen's *Zero* was shortlisted for the Oxford-Weidenfeld Translation Prize in 2019, and her translation of Agnes Ravatn's *The Bird Tribunal* won an English PEN Translates Award in 2016.

MARIE AUBERT

GROWN

UPS

TRANSLATED FROM THE
NORWEGIAN BY ROSIE HEDGER

PUSHKIN PRESS

Pushkin Press
71–75 Shelton Street
London WC2H 9JQ

First published by Forlaget Oktober AS, 2019
Published in agreement with Oslo Literary Agency
English translation © 2021

GROWN UPS was first published as *VOKSNE MENNESKER* by Forlaget in Norway, 2019

First published by Pushkin Press in 2021
This edition published in 2022

This translation has been published with the financial support of NORLA

1 3 5 7 9 8 6 4 2

ISBN 13: 978-1-78227-708-8

Designed and typeset by Tetragon, London
Printed and bound in the United States of America

www.pushkinpress.com

GROWN UPS

OTHER PEOPLE's children, always, everywhere. It's always worse on the bus, when I'm trapped with them. My back is sweaty and I'm feeling irritable. The sun streams through the dirty windows, the bus has been full since we left Drammen, and more people pile on in Kopstad and Tønsberg and Fokserød, they're forced to stand in the aisle, swaying as they hold on tight, in spite of the supposed guarantee of a seat for every passenger. In the seat behind me, a father sits with his child, a boy of about three, maybe, he's watching videos on an iPad with the sound turned up, garish children's animations. The music is loud and tinny, the father tries to turn the volume down every so often but the boy howls crossly and turns it back up again.

I feel queasy after trying to read my book, and the battery on my phone is almost dead, so I can't listen to a podcast either, all I can hear are the plinky-plonks of the metallic-sounding melodies. As we approach the Telemark tunnel, I can no longer hold my tongue and turn to face the father, he's a young hipster sort with a beard and a stupid little man bun. I flash him a wide smile and ask if he could turn the sound down just slightly, please. I can hear the snappiness in my tone, he can tell that part of me is relishing this, but they can't sit there on a full express bus in July with the sound blaring like that, they just can't.

'Uh, sure,' the hipster dad says, then rubs his neck. 'I mean, is it bothering you?'

He speaks with a broad Stavanger accent.

'It's a bit loud,' I reply, still smiling.

He snatches the iPad from his child's hands with a surly look on his face and the boy starts wailing at the top of his lungs, surprised and furious. The old couple sitting in front of me turn around and flash me a dismayed expression, not the child and his father, but me.

'That's what happens when you won't let me turn the sound down,' his father says. 'It's bothering the lady, so you can't watch anymore.'

The bus turns into the petrol station, where it's scheduled to stop for a comfort break and coffee stop, and the boy lies prostrate across the seats, wailing, as I pick up my bag and hurry down the aisle leaving the sound of crying behind me.

Kristoffer and Olea are waiting at Vinterkjær. Marthe isn't with them. Kristoffer is so tall, Olea so short. She's due to start school in the autumn, I think she looks far too little for that, slim and delicate.

'It's good to see you,' Kristoffer says. He gives me a long hug, wrapping his arms around me and squeezing me tight.

'You too,' I say. 'Look how long your hair is now, Olea,' I say, tugging gently on her ponytail.

'Olea learnt to swim yesterday,' Kristoffer says.

Olea grins, revealing a gap where four top teeth had once been.

'I swam without Daddy holding onto me,' she says.

'Wow,' I say, 'did you really? That's brilliant.'

'Marthe took a picture,' Olea says. 'You can see it when we get back.'

'I'm guessing that Marthe was lounging around by the water's edge,' I say, putting my bag in the boot of the car.

'Yes,' Olea says, looking delighted in the back seat. 'She was being really, really lazy.'

'We don't say things like that, Olea,' Kristoffer says, starting the engine. 'You know that.'

I turn to look at Olea and wink, whispering to her:

'Marthe *is* a bit lazy.'

Kristoffer clears his throat.

'I'm allowed to say it,' I say. 'I've got special permission to make jokes about that sort of thing.'

It's so tempting, it does Marthe good to be given a kick up the bum every now and then, and it's so nice to wink at Olea, to make her giggle and watch as her eyes grow wide with glee at how funny I am. We drive along the coastal road, and I tell Kristoffer about the hipster dad and the boy with the iPad at full blast.

'And people got annoyed with *me*,' I say. 'I wasn't the one making the racket. The boy's dad was really grumpy about it.'

Kristoffer has a familiar scent, it's the cabin, paint, salt water, body.

'It's not always easy to calm them down, you know,' he says.

'But you didn't let three-year-old Olea sit on a packed bus with an iPad at full volume,' I say.

'Well, no,' Kristoffer replies. 'But people get so annoyed at children, they don't know what it's like. You have to let kids be kids.'

Kristoffer is always saying things like that, let kids be kids, it's important to listen to your body, things like that.

'But there's a difference between crying and having the volume turned right up,' I say.

I realise I'm trying too hard; I'm exposing myself now, revealing that this is something I don't understand, and Kristoffer shrugs and flashes a smile.

'Having the volume turned right up on a *full bus*,' I repeat.

'Breathe into your belly, Ida,' he says, patting my thigh.

I open my mouth to speak, but I stop myself, he'll never get it anyway. I can tell Marthe, she tends to agree with me about things like this, it annoys her when Olea makes a racket. There's something else I've been meaning to tell her too, not as soon as we arrive, but tonight, after we've both had a few glasses of wine and Kristoffer is out of the way, when he's off putting Olea to bed, then I'll tell her.

I WAS IN GOTHENBURG two weeks ago, I took the train there alone, stayed in a hotel and walked a few blocks to a fertility clinic the next morning. It looked like any other doctor's office, only more pleasant, brighter, with yucca plants in large pots and tranquil-looking images of mothers and babies or eggs and birds on the walls. The doctor's name was Ljungstedt, and from his office there was a full view of the gym across the street. I found myself staring directly at people running on the treadmill and lifting weights. He pronounced my name the Swedish way, not like Ee-dah, but more like Ooh-dah, the first syllable lingering at the back of his throat as he tapped away at his computer keyboard without looking at me. He went through the process quickly, at what point in my cycle I'd start hormone treatment, how they'd remove the eggs, the fact that today he'd just be running a few blood tests and carrying out a gynaecological examination.

'Oh yes, freezing one's eggs has become *ever so* popular,' he said, as if he were selling me something, even though I was already there.

'So I gather,' I replied with a chuckle.

Everything felt open, the summer holidays were just around the corner, it was lovely and warm in Gothenburg and I'd reserved a table somewhere to savour a nice lunch with some expensive white wine, to toast the fact I'd be spending my savings on having my eggs removed and banked, on opening an egg account.

'It's a *wonderful* opportunity,' he said. 'If you don't have a boyfriend or don't want children quite yet.'

'Precisely,' I said. 'I was thinking of going ahead with things after the holidays.'

'Perhaps you'll have a boyfriend in a few years from now, you could use them when you're forty-two or forty-three,' he said, tapping away on his keyboard. 'That would be *wonderful*.'

I tried to picture this boyfriend, imagining a tall man with a beard standing there in the office with me in a few years from now. I couldn't picture his facial expressions, but I imagined him putting his arm around me in the lift on the way out, *we're going to be parents, Ida.* One day, I thought as I lay there in the gynaecology chair, one day things have to work out, one day, after a long line of married and otherwise committed and uninterested and uninteresting men, things have to work out, just lying there made me believe both man and child might materialise, just the fact that I was there and actually *doing it* was a promise that there was more to come, one day.

The doctor and I looked at my uterus on the ultrasound screen, he asked what I did for a living and I told him I was an architect.

'You must draw some lovely houses,' he said.

'Well, yes,' I said. 'It's a pretty big company, most of our work is focused on public buildings and that kind of thing, town planning.' I stopped myself, I was meandering into a lengthy explanation of who designed what, but it felt pointless as I lay there, legs spread, apparatus inside me. As I was on my way out the door to have blood tests done, still slimy and cold inside from the ultrasound jelly he'd used, he said that we'd speak again in two weeks' time, once the results were in, and that we'd make a plan about when to begin, when everything would begin.

I CHECK MY PHONE, no missed calls from any Swedish
numbers. Kristoffer takes the bends at high speed, I feel
slightly queasy and try to avert my gaze from a half-full bottle
of Fanta and an empty crisp packet lying at my feet. He's
grown stouter, his cheeks rounder, I wonder if he and Olea
sit in the car and secretly make their way through snacks and
soft drinks together when Marthe isn't around. His arms are
tanned. Marthe told me they had a few nice days to begin
with, they'd ventured out to the little islands and had been
swimming several times, but it's been changeable since then,
so I've packed both my swimsuit and my woollen jumper.

'When are Mum and Stein coming?' I ask.

'Tomorrow,' he says. 'It'll be nice to have an evening to
ourselves tonight. Marthe's not quite herself.'

'Oh joy,' I reply.

'You know how it is,' Kristoffer says, scratching at his
beard. '*Hormones.*'

He says it in a way that suggests I understand, *you know
how it is*; he knows perfectly well that I've got no idea what
it's like, but still I nod, *sure, I get it.*

'Poor Marthe,' I say, crossing my arms so my fingertips reach my sweaty armpits. I try to work out if I smell.

They've been trying for three years straight, ever since they got together. Marthe has had two miscarriages. She can't keep it to herself, I know as much as she does about the whole thing, when she's got her period, when she's ovulating. It's all we talk about whenever we're together, whenever we see Mum, Marthe talking and crying, telling us she can't take it anymore, that she doesn't just want to be a stepmother, but nobody says *stepmother* anymore, Marthe, Mum says, stroking her back, you're part of a big bonus family, that's what they call it these days, bonus family, Marthe repeats, where's *my* bonus, it'll work itself out eventually, I say, stroking her back too, Mum and I both telling her it'll work itself out eventually, the same thing every time, but *when* exactly, Marthe shouts.

Occasionally I chat to my colleagues over lunch about my younger sister stressing out about becoming pregnant, I tell them that I don't know how she does it, there must be other things to spend your days thinking about, instead of just endlessly trying to make it happen.

When we pull up outside the cabin, I sit up in my seat.

'Have you two been painting?' I ask.

'Yep,' Kristoffer says. 'Well, mostly me, to be honest. It looks nice, right?'

'It does,' I reply. 'Really nice.'

They've painted the cabin white. It's always been yellow, the yellow cabin, it's what I've always told people, we're the ones with the yellow cabin. Now it looks like every other cabin around here, ordinary.

Kristoffer takes my bag. I tell him I can carry it myself, I'm not like Marthe, who wants Kristoffer to help her with every little thing, but Kristoffer says *it's fine* and takes it anyway. Olea runs ahead of us, over the gravel and up the garden path, stone slabs flanking the hedge. She runs everywhere, as if some great amusement always awaits her somewhere up ahead. When I was younger, the hedge was a thick, dense cedar, but Mum replaced it with mock orange a few years ago, she'd wanted something a bit more delicate.

Marthe walks out onto the steps, she looks tired and rubs her face. I smirk.

'Have you been to collect Aunt Ida, eh?' she asks, ruffling Olea's hair. Olea steps back, wriggling free from Marthe's grasp and running away. Marthe knows that I don't like to be called *Aunt Ida*, but she says it anyway. I picture the illustrations from Elsa Beskow's children's stories, the Swedish classics about Aunt Green, Aunt Brown and Aunt Lavender, imagine something shrivelled up, creaky.

We hug.

'Hi,' Marthe says.

'Hey, old friend,' I say. 'It's good to see you.'

Marthe smells nice, familiar, it's almost as if it is my own scent I'm smelling. Her hair is lighter in colour, it doesn't look completely natural, and it's been cut in a style I remember being fashionable a few years ago.

'This is nice,' I say, lifting it up as I run my fingers through it.

'Do you think so?' Marthe asks. 'I think the colour is a bit too light.'

'Not at all, you look pretty,' I tell her.

People think I'm prettier than Marthe, they always have, and Marthe has a complex about her nose and her boobs, so she perks up when I tell her she's pretty. She's easy to please, you just have to drop in a few compliments.

Kristoffer follows Olea around behind the cabin, Marthe and I go inside. The door creaks slightly, it has the same familiar scent, summers long past, old woodwork.

'Ready for the big day?' she asks as I haul my bag into the tiny bedroom, the one I always sleep in.

'Yes and no,' I reply. 'Definitely ready for some wine, at least.'

'Do we have to say anything?' Marthe asks, sitting on my bed. 'Give a speech or anything?'

'Doubt it,' I say. 'But I've prepared something, just in case.'

'Super-daughter,' Marthe says with a smile, the corners of her mouth drooping downwards slightly. 'I haven't had the energy to tackle that particular task.'

I take off my shoes, my feet are sweaty. I feel a pang when she calls me super-daughter, it shouldn't feel that way, she's just jealous.

'But I don't know if I should say anything to her *and* Stein,' I tell her. 'She won't be expecting it, surely? Should I be talking for both of us?'

'A toast to Mum and *Franken*stein,' Marthe says, raising her hand as if holding a glass.

'Stein's nice, Marthe,' I reply, laughing.

Marthe chuckles.

'To Mum and *Ein*stein,' I say.

We're celebrating Mum's sixty-fifth birthday tomorrow evening, Marthe and Kristoffer and Olea and me and Mum and Stein, we're all going to eat prawns and drink wine. Mum said it could double up as a celebration for my fortieth too, I told her that wasn't necessary, it's three months too late for it anyway. I didn't do much to celebrate on the day, just went out with a few friends, we had a three-course dinner and a few glasses of wine and that was that, most of them had to get home to their kids. When Mum turned forty at some point back in the Nineties, she received a card that said, 'Life begins at forty!' I remember it to this day, it was decorated with rockets and shooting stars. Mum liked it and found it amusing, she kept coming back to that phrase all year, *life begins at forty!* she would say, and her friends would raise a glass. I remember them as ladies of a certain age, women with dry lipstick and school-age children, and when they got together, they would call it a girls' night. When I turned forty, I felt the same as I always had, I had no sense that *this* would be when life began. On my birthday, a friend told me that I looked good, as if it were some kind of consolation; immediately after she had said how nice it must be to be alone, because it allowed one to really get to know oneself, and I remember thinking to myself that it might be nice to get to know someone else, too.

Stein and Mum have been together for six years now. Whenever he's due to join us somewhere, I still wish he'd stay at home, that it could just be us. He doesn't have any children of his own, I can't picture him ever having wanted it any other way, and it's as if he doesn't really understand how old Marthe and I are, he talks to us like teenagers. Mum says that she and Stein are *late bloomers*. Marthe and I flinch whenever she says it. It's not even true, she was twenty when she married Dad, and look at how that turned out. I often want to ask if she'd rather have ended up like me, ended up, I think to myself, I can't think about myself as *ending up* one way or another, as if everything's over and done with, nothing is over and done with, you have to tell yourself that the best is yet to come, but at times I think that's how Stein and Marthe and Kristoffer see me. They don't know anything, I think to myself, I've got a plan, I've got a secret. I make up my mind to tell Marthe now, not to wait until this evening, I can tell her now, I'm going to freeze my eggs in Sweden, she'll look at me wide-eyed and say *wow*.

'So, what if I were to tell you I had some big news?' Marthe says.

There's something different about her expression, something serious beneath her smile, something quivers there. I look at her for a few seconds without getting it, but then I do.

'Really?' I ask.

'Really,' Marthe says, she's smiling now, her eyes widen, tearful.

'Wow,' I say, sitting down on the bed beside her. 'Really.'

As she sits there, waiting to say the words, I try to remember everything I've ever said to her, every stupid thing I've said, blabbing away about nights out and Stein and Mum. I quickly embrace her, she sobs gently, I hear a squeaking sound that seems to come from deep within her.

'Fifteen weeks,' she says without my asking, she sits up straight and dabs at her eyes. 'I didn't dare say anything before we could be absolutely sure.'

'Shit,' I say.

I don't know what else to say. I'm so used to consoling her, hugging her and stroking her back and telling her everything will work itself out, taking her out to a bar every so often and buying her a few glasses of wine so she can think about something else, we have to enjoy the fact you can still have a drink, Marthe, and Kristoffer and Mum are always saying how good I am at talking Marthe around, looking after her. But this.

'Things could still go wrong,' I say.

Marthe looks at me and snorts with surprise.

'Fifteen weeks, it's not that far along,' I say. 'If you think about it, I mean.'

'Sure, but we can relax a little bit,' she says, sharply.

'I'm just saying,' I tell her. 'So you don't feel disappointed.'

'I *know*,' Marthe says.

'My God, though, that's amazing news,' I tell her eventually, serving up a wide smile and hugging her once more to be on the safe side. 'To think, it all worked itself out.'

'It did,' Marthe says, laughing, she wants to be happy, not to argue. 'We were just about to go the test-tube route again, and then *poof*.'

'*Poof*,' I repeat. 'The old-fashioned way, you mean?'

'Yep,' Marthe says. 'Can't beat it,' she says, making a fist and punching the air in triumph.

I laugh.

'My God,' I say again.

'Don't you think the cabin looks good painted white?' Marthe says on her way out of the room. 'Much better than the yellow, I think. More like the ones you see down south.'

I pretend not to hear her and close the door leading to the hallway.

I REMOVE MY sweaty T-shirt and lie back on the bed that's already been made up for me, then gaze up at the ceiling, listen to the sounds drifting in from outside; the window is open, gulls screech in the distance and Olea shouts at Kristoffer to watch something she's doing, she shouts until her pleas start to sound cross, *DA-ddy!*, and he shouts *I'm watching!* in a tone that betrays the fact he's looking at his phone. I can hear a boat out on the water, it's going fast, the sky has clouded over, it's cold lying here in my bra. I don't cry. It always smells a little stale in here, and the sheets are soft and slightly threadbare and smell like fresh linen straight off the line, the mattress is old foam rubber, just as it should be, I've lain in this bed every summer since I was a child. And now I'm here. With Marthe. With her husband and their unborn baby and Olea.

I hadn't believed it, not really. My friends have all over-taken me, each and every one of them, but now Marthe too, somewhere inside I had always believed that nothing would come of it, that things wouldn't ever change, that

Marthe would always be there in need of consolation, that she wouldn't ever overtake me.

She can't overtake me.

I wrap my arms around myself; my skin feels withered and dry, my body is a nonentity, no one wants anything from me these days, it's as if I've ceased to exist. I've never brought anyone with me to the cabin, no relationship has ever lasted long enough for that. Marthe has cosied up here with boyfriends since she was fifteen years old and always took the biggest bedroom, listless, apathetic boys that Mum and I rolled our eyes at, until she finally settled down with Kristoffer and got Olea into the bargain. And me? What do I have?

It's so long since I was last touched by someone, anyone. I try to recall what it's like, hands, skin, their breath at my neck, and as I imagine it, that breath, it all comes back to me, what it's like to have someone come up behind me, hold me, their breath at my neck, it's so vivid, so real. To have someone as close to me as it's possible to be, their breath at my throat, tracing their fingers from between my legs and up towards my breasts. I don't want to think about it. There's no point. I stand up and pull on a clean jumper, then perch on the narrow bed, this tiny room, will I ever make it out of here? Things will get better, I tell myself, everything will get better, I'll freeze my eggs in Sweden, I'll become something else, there's something else out there for me, the best is yet to come, I'm not the type to give up. I stand in front of the mirror and see that I'm in good shape, I'll go for a run in the morning, or out rowing, perhaps even both.

Marthe sticks her head round the door and asks if I fancy a swim, she doesn't bother knocking, and I jump, cover myself even though I'm fully clothed, as if she'd caught me in the act of doing something I shouldn't be doing. She doesn't apologise, she's used to it, thinks of it as her cabin. The idea is that we both have equal rights in terms of the time we spend here, but she and Kristoffer are here most often. They're the ones who do the painting and cut the grass and drive to the nearest town along the coast to buy fresh prawns that they eat in the garden in the evenings, and they pull up the weeds along the path down to the jetty, or rather, Kristoffer does, I'm sure it's him, Marthe might do half an hour's work before getting too tired and saying she needs a lie-down on the sofa. But even then, she's a grown-up here, she washes up the crockery with the naturalness of someone who owns the place, buys cushions she thinks would look nice here, while I never quite get around to doing the same myself. I've thought about spending some time here by myself once or twice, just me, I'll clean and treat the timber decking and weed the garden just as they do, take ownership; I resolve to spend a few days here when neither Marthe nor Kristoffer nor Mum nor Stein are around. But it's so much trouble, hiring a car when I can barely remember how to drive, and then there's the thought of not seeing anyone all day every day, plus, I take the boat out so rarely that I've almost forgotten how to remove the hood and fill the tank with petrol, I always moor it with a strange take on a double knot because I can't remember how to do any others and end up getting told off by Mum afterwards. I'd find myself reading old comic books, *Donald Duck* and *Asterix*, and drinking beer in the late afternoon instead of painting walls, alone and restless and in need of a few Imovane when night fell because I'd be terrified, and by the morning I'd just want to go back to the city, with the feeling that I'd been trying to achieve something that was beyond me.

I find my swimsuit and towel and go outside to wait in the garden. The grass is short and dry, yellow in patches, and there are croquet hoops stuck in the ground here and there, I almost trip over one. The cherry trees droop with dense clusters of unripe fruit, a pale reddish-yellow in colour. I pluck a few and stick them in my mouth, they taste sour, I spit out the stones, firing them as far as I can into the air. Kristoffer is busy trying to hang the hammock up between two pine trees. He looks different now, he was Kristoffer in the car, now he's the father of Marthe's baby, a grown-up.

'Congratulations are in order, I hear,' I say.

'Thanks,' he replies. 'I wasn't sure I was allowed to say anything in the car.'

'Lovely news,' I say.

'Why are you saying congratulations?' Olea asks, she's sitting and heaving her weight back and forth in the swing in an attempt to pick up speed.

'Because Marthe and Kristoffer are going to have a baby,' I say.

'Oh, that,' Olea says, sounding disappointed.

I stand behind her and pull the swing back before letting her go.

'Higher,' she says over and over again, 'higher, higher,' and eventually she's happy with the speed she's picked up and giggles as she reaches the highest point of each swing.

'Look at me, Daddy,' she shouts, looking back at Kristoffer, 'look at how high up I am!'

'I can see that,' Kristoffer says, as he ties the second hammock tightly around a tree trunk. He sits and tests it under his weight, he hasn't tied it tightly enough and his bum sinks to the ground below. We laugh. Olea flies back and forth with the wind in her hair as her legs dangle below her, her mouth half-open, I recall the feeling in your stomach when you reach the highest point, the swing dropping from the sky and swooping down, so totally and utterly in flight that you almost believe that you might soar up, up and away, then the way the ground hits you when you land, always surprisingly solid.

Kristoffer wraps the fabric of the hammock around himself, as if he were inside a cocoon.

'Do you think Marthe will see him when she comes out?' I ask Olea.

'No,' Olea replies.

'Kristoffer,' Marthe shouts from inside, as if on cue, then she comes out onto the decking and shouts again. 'Kristoffer?'

'Don't say anything,' I mumble, and Kristoffer giggles inside the sausage-shaped hammock.

'Have you seen him?' Marthe asks me, swaying from side to side and stroking her belly.

'No, I don't know where he is,' I say loudly, and Kristoffer starts shaking with laughter inside his cocoon. Olea giggles on the swing.

'Come on,' Marthe says, standing with her arms by her sides. 'I'm not in the mood for games.'

'I don't know,' I tell her. 'Haven't seen him. Have you seen him anywhere, Olea?'

'Enough now, come on,' Marthe says, genuinely cross all of a sudden. 'This isn't funny anymore. Tell me where he is.'

I say nothing. Olea slinks down to the ground, I can see that she's a little apprehensive now, and Kristoffer unfurls himself and rolls out onto the grass.

'Wow, I can't believe you didn't see him there,' I say. 'How could you not?'

'Don't be cross, Marthe,' Kristoffer says. 'We were only messing around.'

'I know,' Marthe says, and I can see that she's forcing herself to smile. 'I know that.'

The path down to the bathing spot is imprinted on my body, no matter how long I spend away from here. I know the thorny bush you need to watch out for and the smooth coastal rocks you need to slide across on your bum before hopping off, I know the prickling pine needles piled up under the pine trees that filter the sunlight, I know where we have to stamp our feet because there may be adders underfoot; it has that warm, dry, vaguely acidic forest aroma, and Marthe's back is dappled with patches of sunlight. My feet become a child's feet, my short legs preparing to leap from ledges, I remember being scared of falling here, I think about thistles in my sandals, smooth rocks scuffing the seat of my shorts. Down by the large juniper bush further along the way I am twelve years old, I've got braces that hurt my mouth and I'm wearing a new strappy dress, the straps criss-cross at the back, Mum doesn't like me wearing it because it shows off so much skin, she never used to care about things like that, and I bump into Vegard on the way down, he's older than me and stays in the cabin along the road, he's been swimming with his dad and he sees me for the first time that day, or at least I think he does, he smiles differently, or at least I think he does, and he says hello, he says hello to my strappy dress and I scurry along the final stretch of path leading to the bathing spot on tiptoes, repeat his one-word greeting aloud and feel compelled to leap little leaps with my arms wrapped around me because Vegard from the cabin along the road thinks I'm a grown-up in my strappy dress, and Marthe comes running after me and giggles and says *you look weird, what are you doing,* even though she's the one who's chubby and short and always crying about something or other.

Marthe's skin goes goose-pimply in the breeze as we undress in our usual spot. Her stomach is pale and distended. Fully clothed, she might be mistaken as having simply put on a little weight, but without anything on it's clear it's no ordinary weight gain. I kick off from the rock by the water's edge, the cold closes in around me, I gasp and splutter, spit out salt water. Marthe still hasn't come in, she's standing there with water and seaweed up to her knees, swaying gently with her arms wrapped around herself.

'You just have to go for it,' I tell her.

'I'm not as tough as you are,' Marthe says, sounding a little sarcastic. It's always the same, every summer, I'm quick to get into the water while Marthe takes her time, and then we each make digs about which approach is best.

Sitting beside one another on the smooth rocks by the water's edge, our towels wrapped around us and our blood pumping through our bodies as the sun warms us, she pats her stomach and tells me it's not easy, all this.

'No, I get that,' I tell her.

I don't want to hear it. I want her to be quiet, I wish I hadn't come, hadn't heard about it. Now I can't tell her about Sweden, it all seems so pathetic.

'No,' Marthe says. 'I've always thought to myself that, if it happened, I'd be over the moon.'

She squeezes her hair and the water runs down her arms, she shivers. A gull dips up and down on the waves not far from land, gazing at us with those vacant, angry eyes they have, gulls are so ugly.

'I'm afraid that things will go wrong again,' she says eventually. 'I'm hyper-aware of everything, all the time.'

She smiles briefly, feebly, her lips tremble. I should hug her at this point, it looks as if she's expecting it, expecting me to stroke her and pat her and tell her everything will be fine, just as I always do, but I don't want to anymore.

'And we hardly ever have sex,' she says. 'At first I couldn't face it, and now he doesn't want to.'

'Oh, I see,' I reply.

She looks at me, my arms are wrapped around my knees; I say nothing. Marthe picks at one of her toenails, pulling at it until something comes loose, then flicks it away, *eugh*, I say.

'I can see why he's lost interest when you insist on doing things like that,' I say, I want her to laugh but she doesn't.

'Plus, Olea is being so difficult lately,' Marthe says, her tone is impatient now, she can't conceal her need for sympathy, why can't I give her what she wants?

'It can't be easy for her,' I say.

'Sure, but she has to get used to the idea that someone else is going to be joining the family,' Marthe says. 'Do you know what she said before we left?'

'No,' I reply, standing up. 'Shall we head back?'

'She said, *Marthe, you're lazy, aren't you?* Just like that, out of nowhere.'

I follow her back up the path, my feet are freezing and I can feel my bikini bottoms wet and cold under my shorts, my bikini top leaving large, damp patches on my T-shirt, I can see Marthe's vest top clinging to her bikini in the same way. She has Kristoffer, and soon she'll have a baby of her own and still she complains, that's just what she's like, always expecting other people to put things straight for her. Marthe can go around and be herself, she can do an admin job that she likes well enough, which I don't think she's particularly good at, she can say daft things and laugh at all the wrong moments and not even think about it, she can stuff herself with crisps and chocolate when she's feeling down, give up on exercise, say she can't be bothered with it, but there's always someone there to comfort her.

Just before we make it back, where the path gets steeper, Marthe stops in front of me and closes her eyes.

'I need a minute,' she says.

'Are you in pain, is it your stomach?' I ask, and she nods.

I stand behind her in silence and wait. I don't want to ask her how she's feeling, I clench one fist as tight as I can. It's something that happens every now and then, when I talk to Mum on the phone and she tells me she feels sorry for Marthe, trying so hard to get pregnant, and it's like a blow to the chest, to the head, so forceful and hot that I have to clench my fists, sometimes I pick up a pillow or something soft and throw it at a wall as I carry on our conversation with the same old murmurs, *mmm* and *uh-huh* and *yeah*, but it's never quite enough, after I hang up I chuck something harder, something that lands with a clatter, like a shoe or even my phone, if I'm not thinking. Always Marthe. Always. Always Marthe.

Marthe almost always has stomach pains, she has Crohn's disease. They removed a section of her bowel ten years ago, but not so much that she needed a stoma. She went in for surgery on my thirtieth birthday, I'd booked a bistro with two friends also celebrating their birthdays, and when we'd found out the date of Marthe's operation, Mum wanted me to cancel, surely we could have a party at a later date, what if something were to happen in surgery and I was drunk or they couldn't get through to me? Could you ever forgive yourself, Mum asked me. It hit home, but I didn't want to cancel, I didn't want to shift the party for Marthe's sake, it wasn't a risky operation, and I didn't want to spend hours on end in some waiting room leafing through interior design magazines and drinking hot chocolate from a vending machine as I consoled Mum, I wanted to drink wine, I wanted to be in the company of others. Even so, I couldn't shake what Mum had said about forgiving myself, and even though I'd bought a new dress and had enjoyed so much prosecco that I was drunk by ten o'clock, I checked my phone constantly, I was on it all night long. Not one message came through to tell me how things had gone, the operation should have been over and done with hours earlier. I knew that Mum was punishing me, but still my palms felt clammy, I tried calling her but she wouldn't pick up, and I felt certain that something had gone wrong after all, that they hadn't had a chance to call me, that there was no signal wherever they were, I went outside and tried calling from there, stood on the pavement not far from my friends, who were smoking, and felt as if the ground was collapsing beneath my feet, and I stood there, drunk, sobbing, Mum not picking up, until eventually I hung up. I pictured Marthe on the operating table in an oxygen mask, blood and beeping sounds, desperate doctors crowding around her, that this was the operation that would be the anomaly, the one that almost always goes to plan, and that Mum wouldn't call me because I'd chosen not to be there, I'd chosen to go out drinking instead, to do stupid things. I reached out a hand to hail a taxi, it was a light summer evening and I left the party, not to go to the hospital, I couldn't go there now, not drunk like this, but home, where I curled up under the covers after throwing up, shaking, black inside. I woke the next day to a message from Mum to say everything had gone well, and another from my friend asking why I'd left so early without my jacket.

'Are you all right?' I ask eventually.

Marthe takes a deep breath, her eyes are half-open. A gull screeches somewhere, *caaaw caaaw caaaw*. My jaw is stiff, she looks so stupid, she looks so fucking stupid standing there like that, I can't even look at her.

K RISTOFFER TAKES some raw meat out of the fridge and chops some herbs for a marinade. Over the past year or so he's started making sausages from scratch and complicated casseroles that cook for hours at a time and sourdough starters that stink out the fridge, and back at home he has enormous kitchen appliances and a meat grinder and a sous vide machine that dominates the kitchen worktop, Marthe says she's got no idea what you're supposed to do with any of his fancy bits of equipment. He brewed his own beer once too, but nobody liked it much.

'I need some help from one of you,' he said.

'Ida can do it,' Marthe says, stretching her legs. 'I think I'm going to chill out for a bit.'

There's something about their tone when they speak to one another, their words sound rehearsed.

'Is that OK?' Kristoffer asks, looking at me.

'Sure,' I reply.

I don't need to rest, nobody needs to feel sorry for me, and I like spending time alone with Kristoffer anyway, doing something or other as we chat. I grab a knife and slice potatoes into wedges, he admires how quickly I work. The cabin kitchen is small. I used to know where everything was kept, but Kristoffer and Marthe have moved things around, the spices and salt are in the cupboard rather than on the shelf above the hob. They've painted the walls here too, they used to be green, now they're a deep blue, very contemporary, they change all sorts without checking with me first. The windows are the same as ever, the glass panes are old and make the world outside appear warped and wavy, with the odd dead winter fly on the windowsill.

'How did it go with that guy you were going to meet?' Kristoffer asks as I tip the wedges into a roasting tin.

'Who?' I ask him. 'Oh, him. That was just a Tinder date; nothing came of it.'

'You should check out whether there are any hunks in the neighbourhood while you're here,' he says.

I smile, can't face it, can't face this conversation, being optimistic and ready to meet 'hunks', my arms feel weak and heavy at the thought. Swiping left and right, Petter 42, Thomas 36, Steven 45, a beer in a pub where there's no risk you might bump into someone you actually know, that weird shyness when I realise which of the men there is him, he looked different in his pictures. Probing conversations as I drink more quickly than I ought to, worrying about the prospect of conversation drying up, and so I smile more than usual, speak more quickly, gesticulate, nervous that he might start to feel bored, and somewhere inside I think *calm down, don't do that.* Do you watch *Game of Thrones*, I ask, do you watch anything else, what season are you on, is your job very hectic, how many people are there in your department, why aren't I better at this, I'm not usually this stupid. He can see how much more I want, he can tell I've never had a proper boyfriend. Eventually the moment arrives when I ask if we should have another pint and he tells me he's got an early start the next day, and my heart sinks, we might walk a block together before one of us turns off, and I stand there on tiptoes as we make small talk, I know that my eyes are too wide, my smile too broad. I hope he'll tell me he wants to see me again, I hope even though I've been bored stiff all night, but then he just says that it's been nice, have a good evening, then *maybe speak to you again sometime,* and I lift my arms halfway in some attempt at a hug, but he steps back and my arms sink, and then I say *bye for now,* and I lift my hand stupidly in something resembling a wave instead, walk to the bus with my stupid arms hanging down by my stupid sides, sit on the bus alone with my stupid arms, people all around me, make my way into my flat with my stupid, useless hands.

'Make the most of it while you can,' Kristoffer says, wiping his brow, he's melting butter in a pan and adding flour. 'Before you know it, you'll have a husband and kids and find yourself dreaming about how things used to be.'

'Do *you* dream about how things used to be?' I ask him.

'Sometimes, maybe,' Kristoffer says, laughing.

'I'll tell Marthe that,' I say.

'Don't do that,' Kristoffer says, laughing louder. 'Please. That'd make her miserable. But all that online dating stuff,' he says, shaking his head. 'I don't think I could be bothered with all that. It seems like a right fucking ordeal.'

I say nothing, it's easy for him to say, what would he do if he were me, and he looks up from the pan and in my direction.

'That's easy for me to say, of course,' he adds, patting my shoulder.

'It'll be all right,' I say, wasting no time in following up with a laugh.

I chop fennel and carrots. He's nice, Kristoffer, I think to myself. He's a nice guy. As I slide the vegetables into the oven with the potato wedges, I hear a thump, then Olea, wailing from the bathroom. She comes running into the kitchen and throws herself into Kristoffer's arms. Just behind her is Marthe, red-faced.

'She slammed the door on my head,' Olea shouts.

'I was on the loo, and she just barged in,' Marthe says. 'I was only trying to close it, Olea, you know that.'

'Couldn't you be a bit more careful?' Kristoffer says, loud and angry. 'Fucking hell.'

He lifts Olea up with one arm, as if she were a much smaller child. Olea hides her face, nuzzling against his shoulder and sobbing, loud and over-the-top as he strokes the back of her head. It's embarrassing but also not entirely unpleasant hearing her cry like that, Marthe rolls her eyes at me, but I don't return the look. I pick up the knife and rinse it under the tap just to give myself something to do, my pulse is racing.

'You're stupid,' Olea says.

Marthe opens her mouth and closes it again, she strokes

her belly, barely there.

'Olea,' Kristoffer says. 'Stop that. We don't say things like that.'

'I didn't mean it,' Marthe says. 'Olea.'

'Could you say sorry?' Kristoffer says, I can't tell initially whether he's talking to Marthe or Olea. Olea shakes her head.

'How about if Marthe does the same?' Kristoffer suggests. Marthe looks at him.

'But it was an accident,' she says.

'I know, but still,' Kristoffer says, gesturing at Olea's back.

I place the knife down and move over to Olea, stroking her back.

'Want to come out into the garden, Olea?' I ask. 'You and I can find something to do outside.'

I feel a flicker of delight when Olea nods and slides out of Kristoffer's arms, taking my hand, sullen and stand-offish as she continues to refuse to look at Marthe. Kristoffer looks grateful. As I close the door behind us, I hear raised voices once again in the wake of the brief silence.

O LEA AND I SIT inside the playhouse, the one Marthe and I used to fight over when we were young, chasing each other out of it and crying to Mum that the other was being unfair. It has also been painted white, it used to be red and inside there are two small benches and an old foam-rubber mattress in the centre, a box of sparkly dressing-up clothes and a few books and games lying around. Drawings have been pinned to the walls. I used to have a box of things I'd found in here, empty snail shells that smelled of salt and old seaweed, pretty stones that felt smooth and round against a cheek, Marthe and I would take it in turns using them to stroke the other's cheeks, plus a picture of Princess Diana that I'd cut out of some magazine or other, a few nice nap-kins, I think I can remember the pattern on one of them, purple and pink, glossy and soft. Marthe had found the box a few years earlier, I'd texted her permission to chuck it out.

'You can sleep in here, you know,' I said. 'I did once.'

'*Did* you?' Olea asks. 'Why?'

'I used to come here when I was younger, too,' I tell her, sitting on one of the benches as Olea plonks her bum down on the mattress and starts brushing the rainbow-coloured hair of an old pink My Little Pony toy, there are several lying beside it. I remember what the pony smelled like when I first got it, fresh, supple plastic, its rainbow-coloured mane smooth and shiny. Now its nylon hair is thin, the plastic is peeling and discoloured, all of the ponies should really have been thrown out by now, the plastic is probably toxic. One of them is missing a leg, it looks as if it's been gnawed at by a mouse.

'The cabin belongs to Marthe and me, you know,' I tell her.

'Does it?' Olea says, carrying on with her brushing.

What did she think, that I was just some sort of guest? I sit and look at her, her pink jumper, her fair hair. She has dark, even eyebrows, she doesn't look like any of us, not even like Kristoffer, he says she takes after her mother.

'You're going to be pretty when you grow up,' I say.

She casts the briefest of glances up at me before looking back down at the pony.

'How old are you?' I ask.

'Six,' Olea says.

'Are you looking forward to starting school?' I ask her.

'Yes,' Olea says. 'How old are you?' she asks after a pause.

'Forty,' I say.

'Woah,' she says. 'That's a lot.'

'Are you excited about becoming a big sister?' I ask.

She looks at me with hard eyes and says nothing, just keeps brushing.

'It's OK not to be,' I say.

Olea passes me two horses and starts telling me about them, they both have names, one likes to fly. I'm bored by it all, I want to find a magazine to leaf through, a beer, there's a smell of mildew in here. A long time passes before Kristoffer knocks on the open playhouse door to say that it's time for Olea to get ready for bed.

'Maybe you could read to her while she's having her supper,' he says.

'Of course,' I say. 'Let's read something together, eh Olea?'

'Are you and Aunt Ida good friends now, Olea?' he asks.

Olea says nothing, I can see that she's thinking about something else, but I feel proud, I understand children, I know what you're supposed to do.

I make up a voice for Karsten and another for Petra as Olea sits in my lap in her pyjamas, she's eating a sandwich from one of the old buttercup-patterned plates. Marthe is lying in a hammock with a magazine, I hear her giggling all of a sudden.

'What is it?' I ask.

'That doesn't come very naturally to you, does it?' she says.

'What do you mean?' I ask her.

'You're a bit OTT. *Lion Cub and Miss Rabbit can come along too!*' she says, imitating my intonation, making a thing of it.

My cheeks grow warm and I stop reading.

'Don't stop on my account,' Marthe says.

She lies there, stroking her belly in lazy circular motions. I look at her, want to say something mean, but I just smile, I'm not going to let her get to me. I speak again, using my normal voice, doing my best to maintain it until Marthe goes back inside. Olea stops following along after just a few pages anyway, her body grows tired and feels heavier and heavier against my own, and something good and warm and calm filters through me as she sinks back. It's unfamiliar having someone so close to me, her tiny body against mine, the warmth of her head and her stomach, so soft; it makes me wrap my arms around her and cuddle her tight.

'Ouch,' she says.

'Sorry,' I reply, but she doesn't leave my lap, and I place the book down and rock her and sing quietly as the sun moves and we find ourselves sitting in the shade. Across the fjord, the sun is still out, Mum always says it'd be nice to have a cabin across the water.

Is this it? Is this when I'll feel that shift inside me, is this when I'll know it's *this*, this is what I can't miss out on, *this* is too great a miracle to put off any longer, it's not enough just to have eggs in a freezer somewhere, is it *now* that a sense of absolute certainty will force its way to the forefront, so much so that I put Olea down and go inside and find my phone and book an appointment at Stork in Denmark and set off at once to be inseminated with the product of some Dane who's had a wank in a room somewhere, telling people afterwards: *I just knew I had to do it?* Someone at work did it last year, a woman in accounts, she'd looked ancient for years and it wasn't difficult to imagine her being a single mother. She pushed a pram into work one day to show off her baby, skilfully placing the infant over her shoulder for winding, she didn't look as if she needed anyone else. I can't imagine being alone and pregnant and proud and lonesome as I meander through the city, to work, around my flat, giving birth with Mum or Marthe or a friend by my side, never missing the company of a man, it being enough simply to be that child's mother, just them and me, always, the greatest thing of all.

It was only in the past year that it had really started to feel late. Just before my fortieth I started waking up with an anxiety that shook me from within, *not long now*, it said, *not long now and it'll be too late.* Those around me have two or three children, some won't be having any more, they sit up all night breastfeeding, they're exhausted. Others struggle to have another, but it all works itself out eventually, after numerous test-tube attempts and much frustration, and the new baby wails endlessly and they talk about how much more tiring it is having two than it was having just the one, without realising how obvious it sounds. They do drop-offs and pick-ups every day, and the morning routine goes on and on, they never have any problems finding things to do in the holidays because there are grandparents and aunts and uncles to visit, and the need for time alone as a family too, meaning a trip up into the mountains or a camping holiday or a visit to a cabin somewhere or other, just my friends and their children, it's one of their favourite things, they tell me, just having a bit of time *to ourselves*. They move into bigger apartments or terraced houses with gardens, and sure, they said they'd never move out of the city, but *just think, the kids can run outside and play*, they buy all the things they previously mocked, end up with a garage and two cars and a Weber barbecue that's so big that they feel slightly ashamed at the size of it, but it's nice to have a big barbecue when there are lots of them or when they've got family visiting; life is porridge and burping and stains and wee and poo and snot and lack of sleep, so little sleep, and screaming and endless rounds of chickenpox and tummy bugs and colds for everyone, then a fresh bout of tummy bugs all over again. And every morning they eat breakfast together, three or four or five of them, every evening they fall asleep next to someone, cuddled up side by side, every night they are woken by a child who wants to sleep in their bed, a child to cuddle, a child of their own.

Life for me is the same as it was five years ago, ten, even; I have a slightly larger apartment, a slightly better salary, slightly more projects to juggle at work, slightly duller skin, a few more grey hairs that I pay my hairdresser two thousand kroner every three months to make disappear. I sleep alone and I wake up alone and I'm alone when I go to work and alone when I get back home, I won't moan about it, you don't want to become one of those people who moans on and on about things. But being alone is a circle that only ever expands, and if a boyfriend doesn't turn up, if no one turns up with whom I can use the eggs in the bank, there might be five or ten or twenty or thirty years ahead of me just like this, all the same from here on in.

And yet I sit here in my chair with Olea in my lap, nothing shifts within me, nothing stirs, the wind gathers pace and the trees rumble and I look down at Olea's slender back in her pink vest and pick at a little insect that's landed in her hair.

'You can read me another book tomorrow,' Olea says.

'Thank you,' I say, then glance over at Marthe in the hammock and whisper to Olea: 'It was clumsy of Marthe to hit you on the head earlier, wasn't it?'

Olea sniggers and turns around.

'I'm not allowed to say that,' she whispers.

'I give you permission,' I whisper back, and we steal a glance at Marthe in the hammock. Marthe is wearing sunglasses and we can't tell what she's looking at, one hand is resting on her stomach. Why does she touch her stomach so much when it's so tiny, has she consciously assumed this sort of pregnant body language, has she studied the gestures on YouTube, the way you're supposed to sway back and forth and rest a hand high up on your stomach?

'We're only joking,' I say.

'Yes,' Olea whispers, she claps a hand over her mouth to prevent herself from giggling aloud.

'When you've got a baby in your tummy, you end up looking like this,' I whisper, pulling my head back to create a double chin and puffing out my cheeks.

Olea's eyes grow wide, glee and horror rolled into one at being allowed to do and say these things, and with Marthe only a few metres away.

'Marthe says things like, *ohhh, I'm sooo tired*,' she whispers.

I laugh.

'We don't say things like that,' I say, and then I wink at her.

'What are you two whispering about?' Marthe asks. She takes off her sunglasses, as if she's caught us looking in her direction.

'We're just chatting,' I say.

'It's time for Olea to go to bed,' Marthe says, swinging her legs round and out of the hammock. She's wearing a nice pair of sandals; I feel the urge to see if they might fit me.

'Are you coming, Olea?'

'I want to stay up,' Olea whines.

'Come on, don't mess about now,' Marthe says. 'We had an agreement that you could read for a while, then it would be time for bed.'

'I want Ida to do it,' Olea says, she's holding my hand and swinging it back and forth like a pendulum.

Marthe stands there with her hands on her hips, looking at Olea and then at me.

'Uh-huh,' she says. 'Do you want to?'

'Sure,' I say. 'You and me, eh, Olea?'

'Yeah!' Olea cries.

'You two it is, then,' Marthe says.

Olea sleeps in the little box room next to mine, where Marthe used to sleep when we were young. She has to show me all of her books and cuddly toys and clothes before she goes to bed, she clambers up and down on a chair, pulling things out of drawers. Kristoffer sticks his head in and tells her that's enough messing about now.

I lie down beside her, Olea under the covers and me on top. The room has dark, thick curtains to help her sleep even though the sun is still out. We look one another in the eye in the half-darkness until we start to giggle, as if I were a child, too.

'Ida,' Olea says. 'Can I tell you a secret?'

'Of course,' I say.

'You can't tell anybody,' Olea says.

'You can tell me anything,' I say, placing a hand on the back of her neck.

I wish that you were my mum. I wish it was you, not Marthe.

'I…' Olea begins, 'I've crocheted a present for Grandma.'

'Have you?' I reply.

'It's the biggest thing I've ever finger-crocheted,' Olea says.

She chatters for a while longer, about finger-crochet and swimming the next day, tells me I have to go with her.

'I will,' I tell her, I'm bored with listening to her now, I want to go back out to the others, 'but you need to go to sleep now,' and then I sing her a lullaby. It's a hard one, high and low, my voice crackles and squeaks and Olea twists and turns in bed as I sing. I carry on until I realise that she's not going to fall asleep with me lying there beside her, and in the end, I say goodnight and get up, like Kristoffer and Marthe have told me to. Olea hugs me, her arms wrapped tight around my neck for a moment, then she drops back down onto the bed. I think I've done everything right.

I can hear Kristoffer busying himself in the kitchen, glasses clinking and something frying in a pan, Marthe must be out in the garden. I go into Marthe and Kristoffer's bedroom, don't make a sound, stand by their bed, motionless. They have the parents' room, Mum and Stein will sleep in the largest of the children's bedrooms when they come. It smells of Marthe in here, it smells of Kristoffer, their scents are discernible even with the window open. The bed hasn't been made, there are clothes and children's books and a tube of sun cream on the floor. I pick up a green dress I haven't seen before, it smells sweaty. An inside-out T-shirt is lying on the bed, the stripy one Kristoffer was wearing when he came to pick me up earlier, I take a peek inside the wardrobe, several more of Marthe's dresses and jumpers, some of which I recognise and others I don't, vast expanses of cheap, loose-fitting fabric. Kristoffer's shirts and T-shirts, a hoodie. A pair of large sandals have been left lying on the floor. I slip my feet inside them; they look like child's feet in grown-up shoes. I sit on the bed, on what must be Marthe's side, try on a pair of glasses that have been left on the bedside table. They're a stronger prescription than I'd anticipated. I open the drawer of the bedside table, don't know what I'm looking for, find a few old weeklies, look inside the bag on the floor. I lie on the bed, all the while listening for movement in the kitchen and garden, pull the covers up over me and smell them. It's a better bed than the one I sleep in. They should change their sheets, they smell used and unwashed, bodies, I wonder if they've had sex while they've been here, if I can smell that too, or if they've just been tired and lain side by side while Marthe has talked about how hard it is to be pregnant. Maybe they spoon one another, Kristoffer holding her from behind, maybe he rests a hand on her stomach, her lower abdomen. I turn to face Kristoffer's side, stare at his empty pillow, try to imagine that it's me lying here with him, that every evening we come and lie down here together, the window open, spooning, Olea can sleep in my room, and the new baby can be in a cot in our room, and Marthe, Marthe isn't here. Goodnight, Kristoffer, I say. Goodnight, Ida, I reply.

I could fall asleep here, but I mustn't, imagine if Kristoffer were to walk in on his way to fetch something, imagine Marthe were to come in to get changed, I stand up, realise that I'm freezing, I just want to lie back down again.

'I CAN'T FACE sitting outside,' Marthe says. 'It's too chilly.' I pretend not to hear her, take three plates out of the cupboard and carry them out to the garden table. It's a common topic of conversation whenever we're here, and Marthe tends to be the one to get her way, especially if Mum's here with us, Marthe has a headache or stomach ache or any number of other aches and pains, and Mum says we have to take that into account, obviously we do. I feel a little giddy doing the opposite, taking a superior tone: 'No, let's sit outside, Kristoffer and I want to sit outside.' Marthe leaves the table three times over dinner, first to fetch a coat and then a pair of wool socks and eventually a blanket that she wraps herself up in, sitting in her garden chair with her arms crossed, determined to make a point.

'It's not *that* cold, Marthe,' I say.

'You've got no idea how cold I am,' Marthe says.

The meat is a little overdone, Kristoffer isn't totally happy with it even though Marthe and I tell him it's great, Marthe says she needs her meat to be well done anyway, he knows that; Kristoffer tops up his wine glass three times while we're eating.

'Take it easy,' Marthe says.

'I am taking it easy,' Kristoffer says. 'This is how you take it easy on holiday.'

He still drinks more than Marthe would like, but not as much as he used to. When they'd just moved in together, Kristoffer would often pass out at an after-party and forget to let her know, and a few times he'd stumbled home at around five in the morning, so drunk that he fell over in the hallway. Marthe was quiet whenever she called me to tell me these things. I could tell that she wanted to hear me say that it would all blow over, that she wasn't staking everything on the wrong man.

'You can't put up with that,' I told her, I gave her nothing, even though I liked Kristoffer more than any of her other boyfriends.

'Think about when you have children, imagine him carrying on like that,' I said, I felt hot and spoke more loudly and briskly than usual. 'It's unacceptable, Marthe.'

'*You* don't need to get so bloody worked up about it,' Marthe said.

'I'm getting worked up on your behalf,' I said. 'You can't let him treat you that way. I'd have walked out. Then and there.'

'It's not that simple,' Marthe said, louder now. 'You'd know that if you'd ever been in a proper relationship yourself, that you have to take people other than yourself into consideration.'

'Don't I have proper relationships?' I asked her.

'You don't, Ida,' Marthe replied.

Whenever I talk about someone new I'm seeing, as I tend to put it, my friends and Marthe groan; yet another man who's spoken for, I have to stop seeing men who are married or otherwise attached, they tell me, it's no good for their families. I act as if I feel guilty, *pfff, I know*, but it only makes me feel defiant, the idea that I should go around taking into consideration partners I don't know, children I've never laid eyes on, that I have to be the one taking responsibility for holding back. Should I resist the temptation to reply when I receive a message in the middle of the night telling me that I'm hot or lovely or cool or asking what I'm doing right now, if they can come round, should it be me who reminds them that they're spoken for, should I use my best flirtatious-yet-strict tone to tell them *no, you're taking things too far, think of your wife and children*, when what I really want is for them not to give a damn about their wives or children. To go to bed all alone with nothing but my upstanding principles for company, to embrace myself in bed and think long and hard about just how much self-respect I have. Being good, being decent, leaves me with nothing. It's not as if leaving things alone, remaining pure and ignoring those messages, will ensure that a much better man will pop up all of a sudden, someone true, someone unattached, *who values you for the incredible woman you are*, as my friends once put it. It'll happen when I least expect it, they tell me, always when I least expect it, like a reward wrapped up in a bow, something I'll receive for having held out on my own for so long, a gold medal for long and faithful service. It's not my responsibility, when it comes down to it, I tell them, I'm not the one being unfaithful, and sometimes people in relationships fall in love with someone else, I want to say, feelings can develop even if you're spoken for, but I don't dare air that opinion around anyone else, I know how it will make me sound, poor Ida, going around hoping that he'll leave his girlfriend for her, how naive can you be?

I tell them I'll do the washing-up if someone gives me a hand, and Marthe very quickly replies that she and Kristoffer will do it, I can stay where I am, I'm a guest here after all. I borrow her blanket and wrap myself up to stop the mosquitoes from getting at me, only my hands are poking out. It could be nice sitting like this, I could enjoy it. If everything were different, I could be content here; the half-breeze of a summer evening at the cabin, wrapped up in a blanket, dinner and wine with my sister and her boyfriend, Mum arriving tomorrow.

I don't want it. I feel my airways tighten, I don't want it to take so little to make me feel happy, it's not fair, that I should have to make do with this. I see them through the window. The kitchen is half in darkness; the small lamp mounted on the wall shines a ring of light onto the worktop. I can see Marthe washing up while Kristoffer dries, since he's tall and can reach the highest shelves. She looks up at him and says something before smiling, and he looks at her and smiles back, stroking her hair with one hand, something inside me plummets, something like disappointment. I turn away and pour myself more wine.

It's not right. That it should be so easy for others and so hard for me, I don't get it, as if there's some sort of formula, a code that others know about, one they've known since they were young but which I've never quite grasped.

Kristoffer and I have some more wine later, Marthe drinks apple juice, we recline the garden chairs and fetch more blankets, it's almost dark now and we watch the boats out on the fjord.

'Mum will be moaning tomorrow about all the people from Bærum who've come to ruin the peace and quiet with their noisy speedboats,' Marthe says.

'And Stein will tell her that lots of people from Bærum are perfectly lovely,' I reply.

'Oh, do you know what,' Marthe says, looking at me, clapping her hands. 'I've learnt to drive the big boat. I thought I'd surprise Mum with a trip tomorrow.'

'Have you?' I ask her.

The big boat is twenty feet, not all that big, really, but we still call it that since it's bigger than the rowing boat we use for fishing trips. Mum and Kristoffer and I can drive it, but Marthe has never shown any interest, she's always chosen to stay by the bathing spot or in the garden, reading a magazine.

'She's good,' Kristoffer says. 'A natural.'

'I felt like I ought to be able to do it,' Marthe says. 'It gives you a certain number of grown-up points.'

Kristoffer's eyes are shining, as they often do when he's been drinking, and his expression is kind when he glances over at me, serious in the same way it was when we were in the kitchen together earlier. I look back at him and can't bring myself to smile, so I take a quick gulp of my wine, and he winks at me. I go to the loo and almost miss, I look at myself, my cheeks almost drooping, my face bloated. I straighten up, smile at myself, suck my cheeks in, there. When it's Marthe's turn to use the loo, Kristoffer tells me I needn't look so down in the dumps.

'Come here and have a hug,' he says.

'What?' I reply, laughing, he wraps his arms around me and squeezes.

My cheek is against his, it's unshaven; such sudden intimacy, my chest hurts, and when Marthe comes back to say she's going to bed and Kristoffer tells me that tomorrow is another day, I feel so despondent and I don't know why, there's nothing worth staying up for. I sit alone and drink up as I scroll up and down my contact list, eventually sending a message to a guy I was involved with two years ago now, I can't even remember how it ended, it just drifted into being something else, and then I send the same message to someone I had a thing with even longer ago than that, someone I really ought not to contact, he wasn't particularly special. 'Hi! How are things?' I write to them both. 'At the cabin. Thinking of you.'

No reply. I'm always doing things like that, I don't know why, I'm not thinking about either of them, yet still I paw and claw at people in the hope that just one of them might think about me, respond to me. I lie in bed and stare at my phone. The smell of the bedsheets. My hand on my naked flesh. The knots in the ceiling planks. I've been thirteen in this bed, sixteen, twenty-five, thirty-five.

I drift off, the darkness begins to stir around me; I hear a gull in the distance, the sounds generate wider and wider circles, and the door opens slowly, and something is moving in the room, lifting my bedcovers, and I shuffle over to make room, then we're lying on our sides, I'm naked and a hand slides up towards my breasts, I wake up and the bed is empty and I'm wet and it's silent in the cabin, the light is grey, it's early, I masturbate without thinking and lie there wide awake. I don't know who I'm thinking about, there's nobody *to* think about.

When I sleep with someone, on the rare occasion that I do, I'm like a hungry dog; I undress hurriedly, want the whole lot in one bite, chin chafing against stubble, tongue at throat, hard fingers inside me, smooth skin, the warmth, I want to wrap myself up in all that skin. Afterwards, I inch my way towards them and ask them to hold me, drape a heavy arm around me as I prepare to sleep, but they don't want to, they only want to sleep, and I can't help but ask, beg. One doesn't even want to lie in the bed with me afterwards, instead running to the bathroom two seconds after coming then sitting on the living room sofa half-dressed, waiting for me to get dressed and leave, even though his girlfriend is away for the weekend. I try making things better for myself, ask him sympathetically if he's feeling paranoid, maybe it was a step too far, yes, that's it, he says, and I don't believe him, but I can go along with it, I even give him a reassuring hug before allowing myself to be sent packing, straight out of the front door, tripping onto the pavement in the middle of the night to find myself a taxi home. Another one grunts quietly, good-naturedly, as I do my best to sidle up as close to him as possible, God, give a man a break, and pressed up against my bum I feel his penis shrink, and I can't sleep, the air has that same staleness to it that it always does after people have been fucking, and I get up because I need to shit. I sit in the bathroom for a long while, my arse stinging and my armpits pungent with the smell of sweat, my pussy sticky and sore and with that horrible whiff of rubber and dried-up desire; I glance inside the bin where he's tossed two condoms, each tied in a knot, I see some blood on one and think that it's too early for that, and I shower and return to bed clean and warm, move my damp underwear and the empty condom box from where they've been left on the bed, then lie down beside him, in the warmth, take his arm and wrap it around me again, now I can sleep, and he snores in my ear and doesn't wake and I lie there, unable to drift off.

I WAKE BEFORE the others. It's silent in the cabin, six o'clock, and I'm so tired, my head feels laden and heavy after last night's drinks, but I can't get back to sleep. Eventually I get up and take a run along the narrow path down by the jetties; my legs are heavy, but I manage it. I only see one other jogger out and about, we nod at one another, I'm pleased with my pace. I run faster now than I did when I was thirty, not faster than when I was twenty, obviously, but I'm one of the fastest among us when our office puts a team forward for the relay race at Holmenkollen each year. Lots of us are fast runners, *age is no excuse for idleness*, my boss always says, *you just have to make it a priority*. Marthe has tried jogging with me on a few occasions, but she had to throw in the towel after just a few minutes, nobody can keep up with me, speedy Ida. *Do it, do it, do it, do it*, I tell myself as I run uphill, just as I always do, pushing until my sides burn. I shower afterwards and fetch the keys for the big boat before making my way down to the jetty. I unclip the hood and fumble for a long while when it comes to starting the engine because I can't quite remember what position the levers need to be in and which of the switches I'm supposed to flick, but eventually I get there, then I untie the mooring ropes and push off. The sunlight falls brightly on the surface of the water and everything is as clear as glass and there is nobody out here, it's beautiful.

I chug out past Storholmen and Neset and Tangen, the waves knocking against the bow. A gull follows the boat, a huge bomber plane, it flaps after me as I pick up speed and the wind blows through my hair, I start to feel cold, should really have brought a coat. I bat a hand in the gull's direction and it flaps its wings and soars away.

'A natural,' I say aloud, then feel embarrassed.

I drive until I think there's very little petrol left, past jetties, red and white and yellow cabins, moored-up traditional fishing boats, buoys, gulls, the occasional person passing me by, we wave at a distance, then I take the boat out of gear and breathe, out in the middle of the fjord, lie still and allow the boat to be rocked by the waves. I could have carried on, through the inlet and out to sea. Could be doing it right now. I could have forged ahead, on and on until I could no longer see land, until I grew smaller and smaller, until I eventually dissolved, turned to water, until I became shell and seaweed and stone. They wouldn't notice. Where's Ida? I don't know. She was here not long ago, wasn't she? She'll be back. While they shout for Olea, stick a plaster on her knee, clap because she's learnt how to turn cartwheels, while Marthe strokes her belly and reads a magazine. What happened to Ida? Things didn't go so well for her in the end. Well, they went the way they had to go. It's unfortunate. Yes, it was a sad affair. Where's Olea, can you put her to bed tonight, I can't face it, let's go inside, what shall we have for dinner tomorrow night, who's going to do the supermarket run, how do I look, is my bump getting bigger?

I feel movement below the boat, underneath it, as if the sea is pulling me down, I don't cry, there's nothing to cry about. Do I think that I'm a child, too? I'm not a child. I dip my hand in the water, spread my fingers wide, draw them though loose clumps of bladderwrack and something slimy and green, another type of seaweed, wash my hand clean again. I'm here, I think to myself, I'm here, I'm here. I'm here, I'm not going to die, I'm not going to disappear, I'm here.

WE'RE EATING LUNCH outside the cabin when Kristoffer sees Stein's car coming along the road. Marthe has been in a bad mood all morning, she says she's having stomach pains, and is short with Olea whenever she asks for something, *no, you can't have ice cream, not now, I don't know if we're going to go out in the boat, ask Daddy.*

'You said *Daddy*,' Olea retorts with a smirk.

'That's right,' Marthe says. 'He *is* your daddy.'

'But he's not *your* daddy,' Olea says.

'Doesn't your mummy call Kristoffer Daddy?' I ask, taking a sip of my coffee.

'Yes,' Olea says.

'But Marthe can't?' I ask.

Olea shakes her head and smiles; she has one finger in her mouth and is wobbling a loose tooth.

'Why not?' I ask. 'Tell me, come on.'

Marthe looks at me.

'Can you just…' she begins, tailing off.

'What?'

'Just drop it,' she says.

'Eat your sandwich, Olea,' Kristoffer says. 'You've barely had a thing all day.'

Marthe looks past us, up to the bend in the road where the car appears. Shortly afterwards I hear the thud of a car door and Mum shouting hello.

'Hi,' Marthe and I reply in chorus, like before, like always.

'I see we've caught you in the middle of lunch,' Mum says, coming around the corner.

Stein is wearing khaki shorts and clip-on sunglasses over his normal frames, but now he has them flipped up, it makes him look like an insect. Mum bends down and hugs Olea first, she's talked a lot about wanting to treat Olea *as if she were her own granddaughter,* and every time she looks at us as if we ought to be bowled over by her generosity.

'Nice to have visitors, isn't it, Olea?' Marthe says.

Is this the kind of thing people do when they're with children, say totally unnecessary things? It's as if she were talking to a dog, she and Kristoffer both do it all the time, *wasn't that lovely? Isn't it nice to get our pyjamas on? Did you feel sad when that happened?*

'Well, we've had quite a trip,' Mum says.

'I've been fishing,' Olea says, looking up at her.

'Have you?' Mum says, clapping her hands. 'Wow. What was I going to say? We've been stuck in traffic virtually all the way from Sande. We left this morning.'

'We had to stop at Rugtvedt for a hot dog,' Stein says.

'Stein likes his hot dogs with prawn mayonnaise,' Mum says. 'That was quite something, learning that after six years,' she says teasingly.

66

'I didn't see that coming from you, Stein,' Kristoffer says.

'And then there was a diversion just outside Risør and we got stuck at the lights,' Stein says.

Marthe and I lock eyes and raise our eyebrows.

He shakes his head. 'Unbelievable. Sometimes it really hits you that you're in a very different part of the country.'

'Well, you're here now,' Marthe and I say, practically in chorus.

'You could probably do with some coffee,' Kristoffer says, going inside. Stein ambles in after him.

'And you two, my girls, have you been having a lovely time in this warm weather?' Mum asks, patting my cheek and ruffling my hair, then turning to Marthe and stroking her overly dyed hair and gently touching her stomach, why would she be touching Marthe's stomach already?

'Are you tired, my love?' she asks Marthe. 'You look exhausted.'

'Yes,' Marthe says, leaning in to her.

She doesn't have any problem giving Mum a long hug, sinking into her embrace and resting there in her arms, and I pat Marthe's shoulder, perplexed, we're like a sculpture with Marthe at the heart.

'It's going to be fine,' Mum says, stroking Marthe's cheeks. 'You'll be a wonderful mum, you know.'

I don't want to have to listen to this. You'll be a wonderful mum. I feel a growing pressure against my eardrums, behind my eyes, as if I were holding back a sneeze. Slowly they wander over to the garden table, Mum with an arm around Marthe's waist. Kristoffer has set out cups and pours coffee from a thermos flask.

'Now then, isn't this lovely,' Mum says. 'So, how many fish did you catch, Olea?'

'Three,' Olea says, picking her nose.

'Olea, you caught one fish,' Marthe says. 'You caught one, and I caught two.'

'Leave her be,' I say, smiling at Marthe, a strained smile, one that she doesn't return.

I spill coffee on the table as I pick up my cup, and I move the liquid with my fingertip, across the woodwork, smooth it out. These are new cups that Marthe and Kristoffer have bought, and the table is different from the one we used to have, but it's too big, it doesn't work in the space.

'Where did you get the table?' I ask.

'I think it's Bauhaus,' Marthe says. 'Isn't that right?'

'That's the one,' Kristoffer says. 'Picked it up last year, thirty per cent off.'

'You could ask before buying new things for the cabin,' I say. 'There are several of us who come here, you know.'

'You want us to ask you before we buy a new table, when the old one is falling to pieces?' Marthe says.

'Or before you do any painting,' I say.

'You said you thought it looked nice,' Marthe says.

'I thought it looked nicer before,' I say, taking a sip of my coffee. It's hotter than I thought, I swallow quickly to avoid burning my tongue, but instead it grates at my throat and chest, scorching hot.

'It's a pretty big decision, whether the cabin should be white or yellow,' I say.

'But you're hardly ever here,' Marthe says.

'It's not my fault that I don't have anyone to bring here,' I retort.

'No, but that's not our fault either,' Marthe says. 'You could spend more time here if you wanted to, you visit us once a summer, but you're here, there and everywhere the rest of the time.'

'Marthe,' Kristoffer says.

'What?' Marthe says. 'I'm just saying.'

'I used to enjoy coming here alone, you know, before I met Stein,' Mum says. 'I'd potter about, do some semi-nude gardening. It was lovely.'

'Certainly sounds lovely,' Stein says, kissing her.

'Mum,' Marthe says.

I say nothing, drink my coffee and feel sorry for myself, think about what it was like sitting at the table eating a sandwich from a buttercup-patterned plate while reading Donald Duck comic books, the one with the square eggs, and the plastic parasol base that needed filling with water, dark-brown plastic that burned the soles of my feet whenever I rested them on it, and the glass of milk that I often forgot to move into the shade while reading, which left it tasting vile, sun-kissed milk, Daddy would call it, and the yellow of the walls, the yellow they've painted over. I'm on the verge of tears just thinking about it, it's ridiculous, I can't sit here dwelling on how things used to be, clichéd childhood obsessions, oh, the yellow walls, oh, the glass of milk, oh, childhood, oh, parents in love; it's as if a yellowed, Sixties-style filter descends on my thoughts, I feel drained just thinking about it, I wasn't even born in the Sixties, I can't be carrying on like this.

'And how about work, Ida,' Mum says, patting my knee. 'Still chipping away at things, eh?'

'Yep, same as always,' I reply.

'Anything exciting?' Mum asks, scratching her leg. 'I think I've been bitten already, you know.'

'There's no end of mosquitoes here this year,' Kristoffer says.

'I'm going to be managing a new project in the autumn,' I said. 'A high school in Groruddalen we won the bid for.'

'Oh, wow!' Mum exclaims.

I feel the same mixture of pride and irritation that I always do when she makes out that I'm a good girl. Stein nods and raises his coffee cup in a toast, he still hasn't removed his sunglasses.

'Very good, Ida,' Stein says.

'Am *I* not good?' Marthe asks, she's smiling, posing the question in a feigned, childish tone, but the angry heat in me rises all the same.

'Oh, aren't you getting enough attention, my girl?' Mum says, wrapping an arm around Marthe and planting a sloppy kiss on her forehead. 'What are you planning for dinner tonight?'

'I was thinking duck confit this evening, then prawns for tomorrow's birthday dinner,' Kristoffer says.

'Ida's planning a speech, of course,' Marthe says, smirking.

'I didn't say I was going to make a speech,' I say, getting up, starting to stack the plates. 'I just said I'd prepared a few words.'

'You don't need to tidy up yet, Ida,' Mum says.

I'M HER GOOD GIRL, good when I'm sweeping the food waste into the bin, good when I'm washing cups in the sink and burning myself on the water from the tap. I came home brandishing my exam results, *Mum, Mum, look at this, and this,* I feel sweaty just thinking about it, I fill the basin and start washing up, I played handball and took ballet lessons, went running on my days off from training, and in class I spoke up about politics and the EU and female inequality, and the boys groaned and said *shut up, fucking hell, Ida,* and so I was asked to give the end-of-term speech in ninth grade, in the gym hall in front of all of our parents and my class and the parallel class and the teachers and the headteacher. I spent weeks preparing, sitting up at night writing my speech, practising in front of the mirror, trembling whenever I looked myself in the eye, Ida, the grown-up. I was planning to say that our late teens lay ahead of us and the time had arrived to discover things and have experiences of our own, but that it was also important that we have the chance to make mistakes, because everybody has to make mistakes, it's how we learn, that was something I'd read somewhere and I thought it sounded good, I'd even found a quote: *Try again, fail again, fail better,* that's how much of a bloody nerd I was. I imagined letting the last part, *fail better,* linger in the air for a few moments while the mothers and fathers and teachers and headteacher and everybody in our year thought about what that might mean, failing better, what kind of wise and unusual fifteen year old might come up with that kind of thing, and I imagined someone from my class standing up as they all clapped, and then the whole gym hall would follow suit as I stood on stage looking shy but satisfied, bowing a few times with my hand on my heart, and there in the middle of the audience would be Mum and Marthe, clapping hard, and Mum would begin to cry.

Right before the assembly, Marthe got stomach ache. I stood in the hallway at home with my smart shoes on, all made-up, my dress freshly pressed, not a crease to be seen, not a single wrinkle, but Marthe sprawled out on her bed and cried and squirmed, she just lay there, and I thought *not now not now not now, not right now, Marthe, you can't, not now.*

'Do you think you can make it?' Mum said.

'No,' Marthe said, she curled up and talked into her pillow. 'I can't.'

Mum sat down on the bed and stroked her as she looked over at me, at a loss as to what to do. I couldn't meet her gaze, I wanted to kick the door frame, I'd known it all along, this was always going to happen, scruffy, stupid Marthe with her hunched shoulders and her hair hanging in front of her face and her perpetual puppy fat and the dullest of friends, she would be the one to ruin everything.

'I can drive you there, but I'll have to come back to Marthe,' Mum said. 'You'll be OK, won't you?'

'Yes,' I replied.

I sat by myself beside Tine and her family in the gym hall, among all the families, and when they said my name, I stood up and walked onto the stage and gave my speech, I wasn't nervous anymore, but still I stuttered and the microphone whistled, and when I reached the quote, I read it wrong, I just said *ever fail, fail better,* and then I thanked everyone, but nobody got it. People clapped as they always do, a feeble murmur of applause that had ended by the time I'd left the stage and returned to my seat, and a boy in the parallel class gave me a thumbs up, I'd never noticed him before, but I thought about him afterwards, I thought about him all summer before starting high school, even though he had a girlfriend, all because of that thumbs up, I always fell for the ones who complimented me.

Mum came to pick me up after the end-of-term assembly. I'd wanted to mingle with the parents and teachers a little longer, for them to praise my speech, for Mum to overhear, I wanted my form teacher to list all of my top marks for Mum's benefit. We were surrounded by noise, chairs scraping on the gym hall floor, it was virtually impossible to see the painted circles and lines beneath the feet of the parents and teachers and other students, the pale-blue paper tablecloths flecked with drops of spilled coffee and chocolate cake crumbs.

Mum pushed her glasses up onto the bridge of her nose, she looked unkempt with her untameable hair, she'd made no effort for the occasion.

'It'd be best if we could head off,' she said. 'I don't want to leave Marthe on her own for too long.'

I looked at her, wanted to tell her that Marthe couldn't really be *that* ill, that it was just something she'd made up in order to ruin things, but I knew how Mum would react, so I quickly hugged the girls in my class and bid everyone farewell. I didn't catch sight of the boy who had given me the thumbs up; I walked behind Mum down the stairs and across the car park, I can remember that I was wearing high heels and my dress was short, but not too short, I was careful about that kind of thing, and I sat in the front seat and shut the front door. It was bright outside, a bright June evening and I was done with school, done with lower secondary, anything could happen, and then the car doors locked again after us and sealed us inside together.

I wash the glasses, such a good girl, the water I rinse them under is so hot that they almost dry themselves, then I make a start on the plates. The glasses are the same ones we've used since I was little, they belong up in the high kitchen cupboard. I dry them off and put them back, then I take out two and stick them under my T-shirt, it feels childish, as if someone is watching me, I almost start giggling, then I quickly and quietly make my way to my room, where I place the glasses inside my bag.

MARTHE ASKS MUM and Stein if they fancy a trip out in the boat. She can barely conceal her intended surprise, I feel embarrassed on her behalf at what a child she's being about it, how impressive is it really that she's learnt to drive a boat? Kristoffer and I go on ahead, we make our way down to the jetty with the life jackets, a small, shiny one for Olea, and the old, faded-orange ones for the adults, they're stored in the cellar over the winter months, I feel mouse droppings and dust on my palms.

I pull the mooring rope and board the boat, unclipping the fastenings that keep the hood in place. Kristoffer follows me on board and unclips the other side, we finish at the same time. We fold the hood perfectly and lay it down on the jetty, we're a good pair, the two of us working together, and then we sit on the jetty with our legs dangling off the edge like a pair of kids, waiting for the others. Kristoffer smokes a cigarette. I like the smell, the smell of another life altogether, one lived long ago. He hasn't quite managed to give up but says this'll be the last summer, Marthe says she'll be happy as long as he drinks less than he used to.

'Do you think I should get one of those?' I say, pointing at his tattoos.

'A huge, hideous, Nineties tribal design, eh?' he says, looking at my upper arms. 'Sure, I think that'd suit you nicely. I've only spent about twenty years regretting these.'

'There was a time all the girls wanted one on their lower backs,' I say.

Kristoffer laughs, he pulls out his tin of *snus* and puts a pouch just under his top lip; I use the boathook to pull out a length of line floating in the water.

'You could have a life motto here,' he says, tracing a finger along the small of my back, where a slight gap has appeared between my T-shirt and trousers. I can hear Olea behind the boathouse, I get up, and she and Mum and Stein and Marthe immediately appear. When we're all huddled together on board and the mooring rope has been untied, Marthe takes the driving seat on the right-hand side and starts the engine.

'Oh, Marthe,' Mum shouts over the sound of the engine. 'Have you learnt to take the boat out?'

Marthe looks happy, pleased with herself, she's so proud that I have to look away. She does a good job, tackles the swells in such a way that I still feel the pleasant serenity of the water as it sprays and creates its own patterns and sounds and tiny waves, I remember it well from my childhood and it feels good to inwardly acknowledge that feeling again. I lean back over the side of the boat and stick my hand in the water, feel the resistance as Marthe speeds up across the water. The wind blows through our hair, Stein clings onto his stupid fedora hat and Mum asks him to just take it off, but he shakes his head, he wouldn't wear his life jacket, either.

Olea sits on the little deck at the prow, holding on tight. Kristoffer asks her to come down, and she sits beside me. I smile at her, she flashes a toothless grin back at me, I place an arm around her slender shoulders and tug gently on one pigtail, she pretends that it tickles and squirms. Aunt Ida. Her life vest is dark blue and pink, it doesn't look anything like the orange ones I remember from when I was young. Am I going to be one of those people who talks about the good old days, back in *my* day, are Marthe and Kristoffer going to roll their eyes behind my back, maybe I'll wear sunglasses that make me look bug-eyed and a hat that I refuse to take off when I'm on the boat, but I can do this, I coax a smile from Olea, and I hope Marthe sees it, hope that she's watching. But Mum and Marthe are looking out towards land and Mum is pointing, I think she's saying something about the people out on Storsund having an extension done. Marthe does a good job steering the boat when we find ourselves in the wake of a relatively large boat; I see Kristoffer give her a wink and she grins back at him. I can do that too, I think to myself, I know I can, I took a long trip just this morning when none of you were even awake, it's no big deal.

On the way back across the fjord as we're heading home, the boat begins to splutter. We hear it hawking hoarsely, then we bob there in silence.

'Shit, no, it can't be,' Marthe says.

She's got up from her seat and is standing with her arms by her side, Kristoffer is checking the fuel. There's nothing left in the tank, I took it so far out this morning that I practically emptied it.

'Haven't you brought the reserve?' Mum asks.

'I used it,' Marthe says. 'But I was sure we had a full tank, I checked it just yesterday.'

'Is it Marthe's fault that the boat has stopped?' Olea asks.

'Olea,' Mum says. 'It's nobody's fault.'

I could have intervened at this moment to say that it had been me who hadn't refuelled, but I say nothing, several seconds pass, I could speak up but I hold my tongue, there's something so perfect about their expressions as they look at Marthe, somewhat resigned, slightly scornful.

The boat rocks on the strong waves. We're not all that far from land, but the wind is beginning to pick up.

'Is something bad going to happen?' Olea asks, becoming childish and cuddling up to Kristoffer.

I clamber up and stand on the thwart. There are a few boats on their way across the fjord, it's possible that someone might hear us. I wave my arms and call out to them.

'Come and help me shout,' I say.

'You're not supposed to stand up like that in the boat,' Marthe says.

'I'm giving you permission,' I tell Olea, and she climbs up beside me and joins in, shouting *hello!* at the top of her lungs. Marthe watches us and rolls her eyes, but Kristoffer starts bellowing too, and it doesn't take long for a fishing boat to turn around not far from us and chug in our direction, we all cheer. Drizzle has started to fall, tiny holes in the surface of the water.

'Are you having some trouble here?' the man on the fishing boat asks as he manoeuvres his boat up beside us.

'Somebody forgot to fuel up,' I say.

'Not a clever move,' the man says, laughing.

'No, it's not,' I say, I laugh too and Olea joins in.

Marthe tries smiling, her face is dark. She's taken a seat at the front of the boat, tells Kristoffer that he can take over. The man in the fishing boat gives us some petrol, Stein offers him money but he won't hear of it. He waits for Kristoffer to start the engine and gives him a thumbs up.

'Mind you don't forget the reserve next time,' he shouts over to Marthe as the boats glide off in their different directions, and Marthe forces a smile.

Once we've docked, she tells us she's feeling queasy in an anguished tone, asks Kristoffer and Stein to help her back onto land.

'You don't look too well,' Mum says. 'Maybe you should have a lie-down.'

'Yes, I think so,' Marthe agrees, swaying from side to side as she massages her lower back.

My legs are steady even though I feel cold after our trip out. It feels like I've won something. But as Kristoffer strokes Marthe's hair and Mum wraps an arm around her waist, I become withered and wizened once again, I stand with the mooring line in hand, ready to moor up, to tie a first-rate knot that nobody will see, I want to throw the line to her instead, *at* her; this was all her fault, after all.

I LIE IN MY ROOM reading a magazine, I'm waiting for the doctor to call me, I want to book my train to Gothenburg, to make a hotel reservation, to decide when I should start hormone treatment, I want to get things moving. The day will come that I have a boyfriend, a day when everything can begin.

It's two years since I last came close to anything like that. I told my friends there weren't any feelings there, that he was just some guy I'd met on Tinder, he had a partner, but that was his problem, as I used to say. Marthe was freshly head over heels for Kristoffer and nestled in the crook of his arm here at the cabin as I entertained them with my stories of married men, Olea wasn't with us on that occasion. Kristoffer laughed, and Marthe rolled her eyes and said:

'That's so typical of you, Ida, think of his family, I can't believe he even has the audacity to be on Tinder to start with.'

'Can't he think of his own family?' I retorted.

But I did think of his family, actually I thought of nothing else. I wondered if he would leave his family, I wondered about it as I washed up the buttercup-patterned plates, as I walked to the bathing spot with Marthe, as I read old weeklies and replied to work emails I shouldn't have replied to on holiday, I thought about him and wondered if he would leave his partner, I couldn't assume so, obviously not, men never leave, but still, it happened occasionally, some did, some people fell in love with someone else. In the evenings I would lie where I'm lying now, maybe my skin had been warmed by the sun, I don't recall it being particularly warm that summer, and I wondered what next summer would be like, wondered if he'd have left her by then, if he'd come here with me. I was a little drunk after dinner and I texted him about sex. I sometimes got the impression that he enjoyed our exchange of messages more than the act itself; when I was back at home in the city, he rarely had time to meet me. I didn't want to think that way, I'd been on the receiving end of so much crap, I wanted to believe this was the real deal. I described taking him in my mouth, as deep as I could, looking him straight in the eye, and he replied with a picture of his penis, I felt the urge to masturbate before replying, 'Wow,' I wrote, I was at tipping point and he had stopped replying altogether, I waited for a bit, thrashed around in bed and stared and stared at the little blue bubbles on-screen, didn't want to come before he had texted me back. 'I'm going to come soon,' he eventually wrote, 'thinking about fucking you hard', 'Me too,' I wrote, 'want to talk?' We'd done it a few times when he was alone, called each other up and listened in before bidding each other goodnight, voices hushed, giggly, as if we were lying side by side. But now he was taking forever, and then he wrote 'too late' followed by a smiley face, a fucking smiley face, and that was that. I remember masturbating until I came, fast and furious, still trying to maintain some sort of flirtatious tone when I replied to him afterwards, something about how we'd have to get together and do things properly. 'Definitely,' he replied, followed by a kiss emoji, and that alone was sufficient to reinflate my sense of hope, and I lay there, impassioned and tossing and turning and unable to sleep until long into the night. When I got back to the city, I couldn't get in touch with him initially. After a while I received a message from him saying that things had gone too far, it had been nice, he'd said, exciting, that was the word he'd used, exciting, but he wasn't cut out for this kind of double life in the long run, and he wished me well and good luck with everything. 'Thanks,' I wrote back, 'no stress, good luck to you too', smiley face.

KRISTOFFER SERVES US a starter of brown trout ceviche, followed by confit duck. Mum and Stein and I lavish praise on him, Olea doesn't like ceviche and is allowed to have a sandwich instead. Marthe is cross with Kristoffer for making something she's not allowed to eat.

'Plenty of pregnant women eat sushi,' I tell her. 'It just depends what kind of fish it is.'

'I think I'm the best informed when it comes to this, thank you,' Marthe says.

I heard her and Kristoffer in the kitchen before he started cooking, Marthe said he was making too much of a fuss.

'You can't confit the life out of everything every day, it takes you hours, and I'm the one who's left entertaining Olea.'

'You're hardly entertaining her much,' Kristoffer says.

I eat the fatty duck thigh and potatoes in their slick of oil and butter and thyme, vegetables in a vinaigrette dressing, load more potatoes onto my plate, I have some wine, top up my glass twice, it doesn't bother me if they think I'm drinking too quickly. The only person matching my pace is Kristoffer.

'How's the love life then, Ida?' Stein asks after the meal. Kristoffer has taken Olea inside to put her to bed, and Marthe is clearing the table, I don't get up to help her.

Mum gives him a tap on the arm.

'Ouch,' Stein says, pretending to be cross. 'Am I not allowed to ask the question? Is it a "me too" thing?'

Mum has slipped off her shoes and is resting her legs in Stein's lap. He is rubbing her feet slowly, they're brown with slack-looking, craggy veins. She never paints her toenails; she thinks it's vain. I think about Mum and Dad, it's like looking at old slides, I see them sitting on our old garden chairs, the ones we threw out long ago. Dad with his chainsaw, in the process of cutting down some bush or other, Mum sighing and complaining about the racket as she tries to read a magazine, the way she eventually ditches the magazine and stomps back inside. Stein and Mum pick at each other like a pair of chimpanzees, Mum asks if he's too hot or too cold, Stein asks if she needs another jumper or more coffee, Mum asks about Stein's back and he perks up at the opportunity to tell her that it's not feeling great, it's really not, and Mum pats him and says that she thinks they ought to make an appointment with the chiropractor, doesn't he think? I tell them that chiropractors are pedlars of superstition and Stein tells me that they work wonders on him. I once asked Mum who the love of her life was, Stein or Dad, just teasingly, it was a few years ago now. Mum said that there wasn't necessarily one love in any person's life, you can make things work with more people than you might think, she said. Then she pondered the question for a moment and said that she probably wouldn't choose to have children with Dad if she had her time again, if she really thought about it.

'It's never too late for love,' Stein says, patting Mum's knee. 'We're just late bloomers.'

'Late bloomers are closet gays who take years to come out,' I say.

Mum laughs, I don't actually think she finds it funny.

'That's not true,' Marthe says, she's finished clearing up and nestles under Mum's arm.

Kristoffer returns from putting Olea to bed, he's brought a box of wine and asks who'd like some.

'Me,' I say, raising a hand, Mum and Stein only want half a glass each, and Marthe requests an alcohol-free beer. Kristoffer fetches her one. I wouldn't be asking Kristoffer to fetch me things if I were her. I'd be much more chilled-out with Olea, take her out in the boat and teach her to fish.

'What are you smiling at?' Mum asks me.

I shake my head.

'I'm just thinking about how nice it is that we have this place,' I say.

Marthe and Kristoffer look at one another, something about their expression catches my attention.

'What is it?' I ask.

'Nothing,' Marthe says. 'It can wait.'

'No,' I reply, 'tell me.'

I hear my voice becoming childlike, *tell me, tell me.* Marthe scratches her nose.

'Well,' she says. 'We hadn't been planning on bringing this up now. But Kristoffer and I have been talking about whether we might buy you out after a while, take on the cabin ourselves. What do you reckon?'

'Ha.'

'You could still visit us,' Marthe says, as if this is something they've gone over in advance. 'You can have right of use, or whatever they call it. But it would make a lot more sense for us to own the place now that there will be more of us.'

'Did you know about this?' I ask Mum.

'Well, yes and no,' Mum says, shaking her head. 'Marthe told me they were thinking about it, but this was supposed to be a chance for us to get together and enjoy each other's company,' she says, looking over at Marthe.

Kristoffer gazes out over the fjord.

'Just think about it,' Marthe says, taking a sip of her alcohol-free beer.

'Does it bother you that I'm here?' I ask.

'You're not bothering anyone, Ida,' Mum says. 'But it might be a better model of ownership. For everyone involved.'

Marthe shakes her head vehemently.

'We can talk about it another time,' she says. 'It wasn't meant like that.'

'We're here to have a nice time,' Mum says. 'Let's talk about this some other time.'

I have another glass of wine, I need to recover, compose myself, I smile and say that we can talk about it some other day, no stress. Mum will adore and play with Marthe's children, they'll spend their summers here together, Marthe will call Mum and ask if she fancies a trip to theirs, and they'll sit here without me, I'm not here. I've known it all along, I think to myself, my hands are shaking, I have to sit on them so that nobody will notice, I've always known it, that things would go this way. I drink more, need to slow my breathing down. I'll freeze my eggs in Sweden, everything will work itself out. Why hasn't the doctor called me yet?

At around half-past ten, Mum says goodnight, Stein tells her that he'll be up soon. Marthe doesn't want to stay up any longer either, she stands up and bobs up and down on her heels for a while and looks at me before walking off, gazes at Kristoffer, it's clear she wants to tell him not to drink any more. She doesn't like to see me having a nice time with Kristoffer and Olea, I think to myself, and I feel a rush at the mere thought.

'Don't you fancy turning in too, Stein?' I ask when Kristoffer has gone to the loo. 'Mum might be getting lonely.'

Stein smiles at me and rocks from side to side in his chair. He's nothing like Dad. Dad was tall and slim, Stein is only a little taller than Mum, yet appears shrunken somehow.

'Oh Ida, Ida, Ida,' he says. 'You do like to meddle.'

'Meddle, eh,' I repeat with a smile on my face.

I never know how I'm supposed to talk to Stein.

'Oh yes,' he says. 'But I think you ought to give the wine a rest for tonight.'

I feel a sense of fury stirring in my chest, yet still I smile.

'I think you'll find that's up to me,' I say.

'I know,' Stein says, waving his hands. 'I won't get involved. But don't sit here all night long, flirting with your sister's husband.'

'You must be joking,' I say.

'Perhaps,' Stein says, getting up. He stretches. 'Let's say I am joking and leave it at that. Now I'm doing as you suggest,' he says and makes for the cabin, patting Kristoffer's shoulder as they pass each other on the way.

Kristoffer doesn't want to go to bed yet, Kristoffer wants to have some more wine with me. We find blankets and jumpers; we're not going inside. We each sit in our own deckchair and I become drunker and my laughter comes increasingly easily. We laugh at things we remember from television series broadcast years ago, things Stein and Mum always say, we imitate them, and Kristoffer laughs and laughs at my cruel impersonations of Stein, he laughs until he has tears in his eyes, I'm hilarious, I go all out. Kristoffer is funny too, he tells me about the time Marthe went ballistic about something or other when they were painting the cabin, and he emulates her tone in a way that's bordering on unkind, but no more so than when she imitated me yesterday. The box of wine grows lighter and lighter and we have to tip it up to keep it flowing, neither of us can remember how much had been in it to begin with, but it hardly matters, the night is still young, we say, the next morning is hours and hours away, we'll cope, now that we've got started we have no choice but to carry on. I have a sort of tingling feeling in my gut, contentment, it's good to drink, something inside me is soothed by it, it wants this and this alone, it's so long since I last wanted to be exactly where I am. We don't talk about them buying me out, I don't want to think about the fact that Marthe asked me about it, about the fact they've talked about it, that Mum has talked to them about it. The fjord is dark, we see the lanterns on the boats passing each other out on the water, the lighthouse blinks in the distance.

'You're amazing with Olea,' Kristoffer says. 'I have to say it, Ida. Fucking hell, you're good.'

He pats my knee, missing the mark the first time. He's drunker than I am.

'It's my pleasure,' I say.

'Well, sure,' he says, stretching his legs, 'jeez, my shoulders are stiff,' he says. 'It's not a given, you know.'

'Am I right in thinking that things aren't too easy between Olea and Marthe these days?' I say.

'There are a lot of things that aren't too easy these days, to be honest with you,' he says.

'How do you mean?' I ask him.

He falls quiet for a moment, then sniffs and takes a long drink from his glass.

'I shouldn't be talking to you of all people about this,' he says.

'I won't say anything to anyone,' I say.

'Ohh,' Kristoffer says, rubbing his face with his hands. 'It's just the whole baby thing. All this trying and trying and trying for a baby, it's been going on for so long now. I was done with it by the end. Just like, I can't face any more of this, you know.'

'But now it's all worked itself out,' I say.

'Yep,' he says. 'It's all worked itself out. So, there we are.'

He swills the wine around inside his glass.

'So now,' he says, 'now I'm not really sure what I'm supposed to do.'

'What do you mean?' I ask.

'I don't want more children,' he says, looking me in the eye, he looks as if he's on the verge of tears.

'Everything went downhill between Helena and me after Olea was born. You have no idea how exhausting it is before you experience it. It's a fucking nightmare. I mean it, you have *no idea*,' he says, throwing his hands out. 'I thought at the time we separated that if I met someone else, we'd never have kids, never take the risk of splitting up before they were two. I didn't want any more kids. I *don't* want any more.'

'How did it happen, then?' I ask.

'I couldn't do it,' he says, his lower lip trembling. 'I couldn't say no. Didn't want to deny her that, you know? You can't deny a woman the opportunity to be a mother.'

'You could always have said no,' I say. 'If she loved you, she'd have stayed with you regardless.'

I'm not sure I believe that.

'I don't think so,' he says, drying his eyes, he's crying and speaking more quickly now.

'Now she's going around trying to get excited about it all, and I'm just… just so anxious, you know? I can't sleep, I can't even touch her. Just before summer,' he says, inhaling shakily, 'just before summer we had dinner with Kristian and Ann, they're friends of ours, I don't think you know them,' – I shake my head – 'no, but anyway, Marthe refused a glass of wine and everyone was like *oooh, something to tell us?*, and we were supposed to laugh it off and keep our secret, but part of me felt like I actually *wanted* things to go wrong for us again. I couldn't even fucking look at her. I didn't want another one. I don't.'

He shakes his head over and over again.

'Have a bit more wine,' I say.

'Thanks,' he says, holding out his glass. 'You can't tell Marthe any of this. You have to promise me. I can't be saying things like this. I shouldn't have said anything.'

'I won't say anything, of course,' I say.

'I shouldn't have said anything,' he says again. 'I just... it all just builds up sometimes, you know?'

Neither of us says anything for a few moments. Kristoffer sniffles every so often. I take his hand in mine, resting them in my lap. I don't know what to say, it'll all be OK, things will get better, something along those lines.

'I saw how sad you were when Marthe suggested that we buy you out,' he says after a while.

'Well, there are worse things in the world,' I say.

'You can say it,' he tells me.

'I was,' I reply. 'Yeah.'

'I've been thinking about what this must be like for you, all of this,' he says. 'You don't say much.'

He's thought about it. He's thought about me.

'Sometimes,' I say, taking a deep breath, sobs trapped inside my ribcage, pushing their way out. 'Sometimes I... I just, I mean, I just...'

I make it no further.

'I just feel a bit lonely,' I say.

He moves his chair closer to mine and places an arm around me so my nose is pressed against his T-shirt. I feel the soft lining of his hoodie, it smells of Kristoffer. I pull my legs up onto my chair and nestle into the crook of his arm, as if I were a child.

'I think you deserve better,' he says.

'Soon you'll be telling me that I should listen to my body,' I say.

'Well, it *is* important to listen to your body,' he says, laughing and sniffling.

'Do you want a bit of my blanket?' I ask.

'Thanks,' he says, and I move my chair even closer to his and pull the blanket over us both. He leans back in his chair and his chin rests on his chest. I rest my head on his shoulder, it's so warm there, wait for him to move and say that we ought to go to bed, but he doesn't, he stays here with his warm body against mine, I let his warmth merge with mine, this is what it can be like, this is what it feels like. We sit that way for a long while, it feels like he might have drifted off. He wants to be here, just like me, I think to myself, pondering the thought deep within my warm, drunk mind where everything is soft, he wants to be here with me. I inch my way up and sniff at the hollow of his neck, he smells nice, safe. I take his chin in my hand and kiss him. His lips are sealed and dry.

'Hmm,' he says, his eyes flickering. He shakes his head.

He wants this, I think to myself, he wants this, he wants this.

I kiss him again, try to open his mouth with my own. A party boat sails slowly by out on the fjord. It glides past in the distance, I can only see its lanterns, but the sound carries over the water, I can hear singing and shouting, the odd word. The music is turned up loud, a Norwegian summer hit from the Nineties, and people screech along at the top of their voices.

'That fucking song,' Kristoffer mumbles, I can't tell if he's muttering the words to me or to himself, and then he drifts off.

I rest against his chest, he's motionless, smacks his lips in his sleep, I stroke his stomach, slip a hand under his T-shirt, let it rest there. I'm not cold. My head is spinning and I hope I'm not going to have to throw up, and I fall asleep; it begins to grow light.

I KNEEL BEFORE THE TOILET and stick my fingers down my throat, as far back as I can, my hand wet with spit, my stomach contracting. Whenever I close my eyes the sense of careening off course returns; I groan and sweat and retch, gripped by brief convulsions before it comes up. Pale red in parts, it must be the ceviche, I gather my hair and hold it at the nape of my neck with one hand, supporting myself with the other, pulling myself close to the toilet and contorting with each fresh convulsion, my eyes streaming. Afterwards I rest my head on the porcelain toilet bowl and gasp at the sense of release, light and empty, on the brink of sleep, nothing can top the feeling of having just thrown up. Whirling around inside my head is that same fucking song, I spend ages in the shower with my arms by my sides and feel myself starting to come to again, I turn the temperature up a few notches, standing there until my skin reddens. I look in the mirror as I brush my teeth. I look old today. Two deep lines run from the outer corners of my eyes and diagonally down each cheek. Still, I'm attractive, it has to be said. Nothing happened, I tell myself. It's safe to emerge, nothing happened. Something inside me quivers with excitement, an illicit shudder deep down in my gut, nothing happened, but we came *close*, it's impossible, but still, we came close.

Marthe and Mum are sitting at the kitchen table having a cup of tea. Olea is sitting on the floor, drawing. It's late morning, and the sky outside is overcast, a breezy day. I woke up early this morning in the garden, bitterly cold. Kristoffer had woken before me and gone inside, the blanket had been left draped over me. I had fallen into bed and immediately passed out, sleeping for a few hours before waking with a pounding headache, my mouth and throat dry. I think I dreamt about him; I need to talk to him.

'Happy birthday,' I say, giving Mum a hug, hoping I don't still smell of alcohol.

'Thank you, Ida,' she says, hugging me back.

'Where are the others?' I ask.

'Stein is down by the jetty,' Mum says. Marthe doesn't look up from her phone. 'Kristoffer is still asleep.'

'Gosh,' I say, forcing a chuckle, ensuring I'm standing with my back to her as I make myself a coffee.

I can't turn around to face Marthe, I'm afraid that she'll see something in my expression. Nothing happened, I tell myself, nothing happened, there's nothing to feel guilty about. I feel an urge to see Kristoffer, to feel his physical presence in the room. We have to talk about what happened, I think to myself, you have to talk about things like that, nothing happened, but we have to talk about the fact that nothing happened, or perhaps we won't, perhaps we'll just exchange looks all day long, well aware that something almost happened, perhaps we'll find an excuse to wander down to the jetty together and sort out the boat. Tonight we'll drink again, we'll sit together as the others make their way up to bed, and he'll tell me that *we* should be together, I can tell him that wouldn't work, that he can't say things like that, that Marthe is my sister, we can't, but how am I supposed to resist, he'll say, you're so easy to talk to, I can't talk to anyone else like this, there's a connection between us, I don't understand how I could have failed to see it all along. Something grows in me at the mere thought of it, delight, dread, oh, it's impossible, but perhaps it's possible, who really knows what's possible and what's not?

'What are you up to, Olea?' I ask, mostly just to have something to say.

'Just drawing,' Olea says.

'She's making Mum a birthday card,' Marthe says.

'You shouldn't say that in case it's a surprise,' I say.

'Of course, *Mum*,' Marthe says, smiling while also managing to look bad-tempered.

'Stop it now, you two,' Mum says. 'Is this about the cabin thing?'

'No, no,' I reply, taking Olea's hand. I glance over at Marthe, but she just shrugs.

'Shall we go and wake Daddy, Olea?' I ask.

Olea opens the bedroom door and shouts *Daddy!* in a loud, dramatic voice.

'Is that my girls?' Kristoffer mumbles, sounding grotty and sluggish. Then he sees that it's me, doesn't say a word, but turns to face Olea. He's not wearing a T-shirt and shuffles upwards until he's leaning on his elbows, his face grimy-looking. It feels like this is something I shouldn't see; I stand in the doorway, wavering, feeling stupid.

'Why does it smell so yucky in here?' Olea asks. She sits on the bed and bounces up and down.

'Daddy's not feeling very well,' Kristoffer says.

'Really?' Olea asks, unconvinced.

'I've been a bit under the weather,' Kristoffer replies. 'But I'm almost better now.'

He wraps his arms around Olea and squeezes her until she squeals with glee.

'Are you my best buddy?' he asks, burying his nose in her hair, playful and warm, jiggling her gently from side to side. 'Are you my best buddy?'

'Nooo,' Olea shrieks, wrangling herself free and giggling. 'You smell yucky.'

'Who *is* your best buddy, then?' Kristoffer asks, tickling her.

'Uhhh,' Olea says, pretending to think about it, pulling faces and cocking her head to one side in an over-the-top performance. 'Um, um… Ida!' she shouts all of a sudden, pointing at me.

'Oh really?' Kristoffer replies, he chuckles and looks up at me. 'Sounds like you've surpassed me, thanks for that.'

'Sounds like it,' I say, chuckling along with him.

'Why don't you head out for a bit, Olea,' Kristoffer says, sitting up in bed. 'I just need to have a word with Ida.'

'Is it a secret?' Olea asks.

'No, just something boring,' Kristoffer replies.

'Why do I have to go away?' Olea asks.

'It's about Granny's birthday,' Kristoffer says.

'I want to hear too!' Olea says.

'It's just about cooking dinner tonight,' Kristoffer says. 'Go and see Granny and ask her if you can have an ice cream.'

Olea huffs and makes a show of dragging her feet on her way out of the room before banging the door closed behind her. I wonder if I should perch on the edge of the bed, but I remain standing, he should ask me to, if that's what he wants.

'Things went a bit too far last night,' Kristoffer says.

'Oh?' I reply, pretending not to understand.

'No, well, firstly, I was pretty out of it,' he says, rubbing his eyes.

'You can say that again,' I reply, laughing. He doesn't join in my laughter.

'Still,' he says, crossing his arms. I try not to look at him too much. There are patches of hair on his arms and a fair bit on his chest, it's curly. Somehow he seems more naked than when we were out swimming, with only the duvet separating us. I realise that I was lying beneath the same duvet just yesterday.

'Anyway, I remember saying a few things I shouldn't have,' he says. 'I have a tendency to run my mouth when I'm drunk, if you know what I mean.'

'You needed to get it off your chest,' I say.

He chuckles.

'Well, sure,' he says.

'I thought it was good,' I say, sitting on the edge of the bed, placing a hand on the duvet and realising at once that I shouldn't have, but knowing that I can't get up now.

'I just need to know that it stays between us,' he says, holding his hands up as if he were measuring something.

'Of course,' I reply. 'You can always talk to me.'

'Quite the opposite, I need to learn to hold my tongue when I've had a drink,' he says.

He looks at me and points, a slight smile crossing his lips. 'And *you* need to learn not to come on to people when *you've* had a drink. Deal?'

'What?' I say, coming over hot and cold all at once, feeling the sweat spread under my arms, down my spine.

'You know what I'm talking about,' Kristoffer says. 'It won't happen again, all that, will it?'

I sit there in silence, a pounding in my head, my ears. When I don't get up to leave, he looks at me and says: 'I think it's time I got up.'

'Oh,' I reply. 'Of course, yes.'

I step out of the room and close the door behind me, the nape of my neck damp with sweat.

M UM AND I WALK to Heia. The forest is dry, dust
rises from the path beneath our feet. I've taken two
paracetamol and thrown up once more, retching as quietly
as I was able to behind the bathroom door, I feel better
now. I know this path well too, know the way it creeps
up into the forest past the white house and meandering a
little too close to the red one, know where you can catch a
glimpse of the sea before the pathway curves back around
into the woodland, know what the shadow cast by the
towering, steep rock above feels like on my skin, it looks
like a troll. It's always cool there in the shade, I recall flat
beetles creeping past my head as I stood against the rock
face, busy playing hide-and-seek and kick the can, recall the
moss and lichen that I picked and scraped off the rock as
I listened for the others, waited for them to find me, earth
accumulating beneath my nails, Mum scrubbing my hands
with the nailbrush when I returned to the cabin in the evening. Now Mum is walking ahead of me on the same path,
a little slower than me, but that's nothing to do with her
age, she's always been that way, just slow enough to make

me feel impatient. Anyone who walks too slowly makes me feel impatient, anyone who talks too slowly makes me feel impatient, Mum and Marthe both have a sluggishness to them. Mum is wearing a cap and knee-length shorts with a pair of relatively new trainers, her hair has started thinning but her waistline is wider than it used to be, and she has a prominent varicose vein on the back of one leg.

'I sometimes think about your father when I'm here,' she says, turning to look at me. 'It's a funny thing. I mean, it's always been my cabin. Does that happen to you too?'

I say nothing. There's a rustling in the undergrowth beside us, it must be a bird.

When Dad died, I hadn't seen him for two years. He would call me on occasion when he was in town, suggest that he and I and Marthe meet at a café, but I always came up with some excuse or other. Dad moved to Tromsø when I was thirteen, and before that we'd spent every other weekend and every Wednesday at his house for the few years after their divorce. That was how things were back then, you never saw children splitting their time fifty-fifty between parents like you do these days. Whenever Mum was angry or upset after speaking to Dad on the phone, I felt a chill within, a thick column of cold that ran from my stomach and up through my chest, I'd run to her and hug her as tightly as I could and tell her that I loved her much, much more than Dad, we don't need Dad, I told her. Or I'd tell her that I wished he were dead, and Marthe would scream that I shouldn't say things like that, and Mum said the same thing, but I knew that she wasn't as angry, she responded with a kind of distressed amusement, as if I'd said something she'd been thinking. *That woman*, I heard Mum say over the telephone, and I started saying it too, *that woman*, whenever I was telling others that Dad had a new girlfriend. His new partner had two kids of her own, he's chosen a new family, Mum would say, she was always saying that he'd ruined her life, crying as she made breakfast, telling me that it was just us now, we have to look after Marthe together, she'd say. When things ended between Dad and *that woman*, when he eventually found yet another partner and moved to Tromsø, I refused to visit him, I was old enough to refuse. Marthe flew there with a tag around her neck, 'I'm flying solo', she hadn't wanted to refuse. Mum and I waved her off at Fornebu airport one weekend a month, Mum always felt compelled to weep as she bid her farewell, she was afraid that Marthe would be taken ill when she was up there and that the doctors in Tromsø wouldn't be as good as the doctors at home. But Marthe would always swagger back, brimming with tales of new friends and the midnight sun, they'd eaten lasagne made by Dad's new girlfriend, and I almost couldn't breathe as she regaled us with it all, because she had experienced all of that, because she travelled unburdened by any anxieties, bright and breezy, and that could have been me. But I couldn't do it to Mum, I had to stay close. Marthe, on the other hand, she didn't understand that her enthusiasm had the potential to upset Mum, from time to time she was unstoppable all the way home from the airport in the car, chattering on and on about how much fun she'd had, and

I was scathing with her, mimicked her cruelly and sniggered at the clumsy northern expressions she'd picked up, and Mum told me not to be mean, but I could tell that it cheered her up a bit, we were a team, her and me.

I never visited Dad in his new house. I was proud of that fact as a teenager, I would announce to Grandma or Mum's friends that I'd never been and that I had no interest in going. I used dramatic turns of phrase, *I'll never forgive him for what he did to us*, and Mum acted as if it worried her, she called it *Ida's teenage rebellion*. Whenever Dad would call, I'd give brief, one-syllable answers to his awkward questions. After a while he began calling less often, and we only saw each other infrequently, meeting for the occasional coffee when he was in town. Even though I grew older, I still felt like a bad-tempered, uncooperative teenager, while Marthe hugged him so naturally, in a way that I could see made him so happy, she continued her trips to Tromsø, and I felt a kind of quiet disappointment about it all, perhaps I'd have been able to do the same, except it would only have been weird if I'd started doing it all of a sudden. But then he got cancer, we hadn't spoken for many months at that point. It was pancreatic cancer. Marthe went up north to see him, and when she came back home, she told me I had to go too, that I'd regret it if I didn't. I didn't think it could be all that bad, things would improve, I had to think about it for a while before going, I wasn't ready. While I was busy thinking, his wife rang to tell Marthe that he had died.

———

At the top of Heia, we look out at the view and point out houses across the fjord that we think we recognise. There are a few people up here. A mother just a little older than me in workout leggings and a crop top is trying to squeeze herself, her three children and her dog into a picture, with a view of the fjord behind them. The two eldest stand behind her, smiling and holding up peace signs as she kneels with her phone in front of her in one hand. They all look at the pictures afterwards.

'You didn't get Malin in,' the boy says.

'Do you want me to take one for you?' I ask.

'Oh, that'd be great,' the mother says, passing me her phone.

I hold the phone up and look at them on screen, the sun behind them, their faces are going to be dark. Mum steps back out of the way and smiles.

'You too, Malin,' the mother says, reaching out for her youngest daughter. 'All together now.'

'But it's windy,' the youngest girl says. 'My hair is blowing everywhere, it's going to look so bad.'

'Everybody's hair is blowing everywhere,' the mother says. 'It's not that big a deal.'

'I don't want to,' the girl shouts, breaking free.

I stand there with the mother's phone in my hand and wait.

'Come on,' the mother says. 'Don't create a drama out of nothing.'

'I don't want a fucking picture!' the girl shouts, on the verge of tears.

The swear word rings out around us, she's young and lanky, wearing pink trainers, she might be nine or ten. I don't know where to look, her siblings smirk.

'Malin!' her mother says. 'Stop that.'

'Malin, you're making an idiot of yourself,' her brother says.

They smile again, I take the picture, then one more, *there*, I say, showing them, and the mother thanks me with a wide smile. I wait for her to tell the girl off for her bad language, but she lets it go. Mum and I laugh about it on the way back downhill.

'I felt bad for the little one,' Mum says. 'But she was a tough nut. There was an air of Pippi Longstocking about her.'

'Yes,' I say, but I think about the fact that I hadn't felt bad for her at all, I'd felt just as delightfully furious as her brother, as if I were an older sibling too, furious that she couldn't behave, that she just stood there worrying about her hair and whinging and moaning and wasting everybody else's time, including two random women, everybody standing there waiting for her. I'd never have done anything like that, I think to myself, I'd have done as Mum told me to, smiled at the woman taking the picture, and quietly relished hearing my little sister being told off.

I'VE GOT A MISSED CALL on my phone, it's a Swedish number. My mouth goes dry and my pulse pounds in my palms as I close the bedroom door and return the call. I get through to a switchboard and ask to be connected to Dr Ljungstedt, telling the woman on the end of the line that I think he's tried to call me to give me some test results. *Please hold*, the Swedish woman on reception tells me, *I'll see if he's free.*

'Hello,' I say as the doctor is connected, and I give my name, feeling my heart thump in my chest and ears.

'Hello there, Ida,' he says.

He pronounces my name the Swedish way again, just as he did when I visited his clinic.

'How are things, Ida?' he asks.

'Well, thank you,' I reply.

'Enjoying the summer?' he asks.

'Yes, thank you,' I reply.

'Drawn any more lovely houses lately?' he asks.

'Oh yes,' I reply, shuffling impatiently on the bed.

His voice is a little unclear on the phone, but I hear him

say that the results of my tests are back, and that things unfortunately don't bode too well.

'I must say, I think…' he says, and then he says something I don't catch.

'Sorry, I didn't quite catch what you said there,' I say.

He repeats it, but I still can't tell what he's saying.

'I'm sorry, you'll need to say that one more time,' I tell him. 'I just want to make sure I'm hearing you properly.'

He tells me that I don't have a sufficient number of eggs to freeze, those aren't the exact words he uses, but he says something along those lines in Swedish. I catch his every word this time.

'Oh, I see,' I say.

I look out of the window, there's a bird dropping on the windowpane that I hadn't noticed before now. Seagulls. A sailboat passes by out on the fjord, a craft with a huge sail. I wonder what it's called, who's on board, where they're headed.

'Have I been too direct?' he asks.

'No,' I reply. 'No, no. I'd rather you were direct. I can take it.'

'But you had perhaps thought this might be the case,' he says. 'You are forty, after all.'

I've started to cry even though I don't want to, there's nothing to cry about, and he can hear it, my voice is thick, my nose sounds blocked, it seems so obvious that I ought to have considered things might go this way, sitting here now I can't fathom why I hadn't, what with me being forty years old.

'I'm sorry,' he says. He'd noticed the small number of eggs during my ultrasound, he explains, but he'd decided it would be better to have the discussion with me after my results came back.

He carries on talking, says something about how many hormone treatments I would need if there was to be any hope of my having enough eggs to freeze, he couldn't recommend it from a medical point of view and, moreover, it would be expensive. I interject, ask him if pregnancy will ever be possible for me. He hesitates.

'There's always a slim chance,' he says. 'As long as you're still having regular periods. But, you know. People ought to be having children when they're thirty, but that doesn't work for everyone, then all of a sudden, they realise they've put it off for too long. It's *ever so* sad, but these things happen from time to time.'

WE HAVE TO SIT AROUND the kitchen table for the birthday meal, it's too windy outside for it to be any fun sitting in the garden. The prawns have been laid out on a plate on the kitchen worktop to defrost, Kristoffer drove into town to go to the supermarket, they were all out of fresh prawns. I wonder if he was fit to drive. He doesn't make eye contact with me, sitting on the sofa with a book, chatting to Olea every so often and asking her to put down her iPad, reading something aloud to her. I wander around the cabin, tidying up, setting the table, putting out wine glasses for each of us. I lay in bed for a while after speaking to the doctor. I cried a little, but not much, my chest felt too tight for my sobs to surface, there wasn't enough air. I tried taking deep breaths and exhaling steadily, but the heaving and stuttering burned inside me, as if someone were standing there forcing my ribcage closed. I trembled and wondered if I had a fever, pulled the duvet up over me even though I was fully clothed. Eventually I could lie still no longer; I stood in the bathroom and googled breathing exercises, tried one called square breathing, sobbed on every inhale, felt so cold that I had to take a shower, standing for ages in the warm water.

We sing 'Happy Birthday' to Mum at the table, mostly for Olea's benefit. Marthe and Kristoffer and Stein sing loudly, I sing softly, there isn't enough air. I'll never be anyone's mother, no grown-up children will ever sing to me on the day I turn sixty-five, I'll never be anyone's grandmother, I'll never have any grandchildren to celebrate Christmas with. A void opens up within me, I stare at the great, black, empty space and sing *happy birthday, dear Mum, happy birthday to you*, I'll never know this myself, it's too late. Square breathing, breathing in and looking up, breathing out and looking to the right, breathing in and looking down, breathing out and looking to the left, I do it a few times in a row while the others are busy chatting.

We toast Mum's health with white wine, Kristoffer pours Olea some cola, he doesn't look at me and he doesn't look at Marthe, I can see her trying to catch his eye too. I'll never pour my child cola. I'll never visit them at the cabin, I'll never have anyone to visit. The water in our finger bowls is cloudy, a few prawn antennae float on the surface. My hands are unsteady, I'm shaking as I peel the shellfish, I can hear myself praising the plump, juicy prawns.

'Prawns are actually at their best in January and February,' Stein says, 'when the water is at its coldest.'

I line the prawns up on a slice of bread and squeeze a Z-shape on top in mayonnaise, then drizzle lemon juice over them and rub my fingers with the wedge of lemon so they won't smell, but I can only manage half of my open sandwich, I leave the rest uneaten. I recall all the times we've eaten prawns here, thinking back to when I was a little girl and Dad would peel them for me, we would make a little pile in the middle of my slice of bread, the memory is painful.

I tap my glass with my knife and stand up, I'm forced to do it once more to be heard over Olea and Stein, who are chatting about Peppa Pig at full volume, Kristoffer shushes them. Mum rests her hands in her lap and smiles, thrusting her chin out in anticipation. It's strange to be standing less than a metre away from the table to say a few words, it feels far too formal to be faced with the expressions they all assume, polite and interested, as you should be when you're listening to someone giving a speech, even though it's just me and the six of us here.

'Dear Mum,' I say, rustling the sheet of paper on which I've jotted down a few keywords. 'It's funny to think that you're sixty-five. Marthe and I are always hearing that we must have good genes, given our mother's youthful appearance.'

I almost sound normal, my cheeks are warm again. Kristoffer smiles and Stein glances over at Mum with pride. Marthe peels prawns for Olea and lays them on her plate as I'm speaking, one and two and three and four.

'It's a funny thing, age,' I say. 'I remember when you were given the card that said "Life begins at forty", that was the kind of thing people found funny back in the Eighties. Do you remember it?'

'Not entirely,' Mum says.

'There were pictures of rockets on it, that sort of thing,' I say. 'No? Well, I guess not, not that it matters that much. But either way, when I was little, that card had me convinced that it would be *exciting* to turn forty.'

Stein laughs. Kristoffer gives the briefest of smiles. I glance down at my keywords. I'd planned on turning it into a sweet story about Marthe and Mum and me, about how I was looking forward to becoming an equally spritely sixty-five year old myself, fawning over her a little, and then I'd wrap up with a quote from the speech they never heard, *try again, fail again, fail better,* but now I find myself looking at my own handwriting and none of it makes sense to me. There's nothing here. There's nowhere I can go from here. Do we know each other at all, good girl Ida, cuddly Marthe, we come here every year and do all the same things, how did we become what we are, what does it mean to fail better, why am I asking Mum to fail better, it doesn't make any sense, you either fail or you don't, she's not the one who's failed.

'So, anyway, happy birthday,' I say, raising my glass, and we have to toast before anyone has a chance to ask if that's really it, and I sit back down. Mum looks confused but smiles at me; Marthe furrows her brow. Stein claps.

'Ida, Ida, Ida, lovely.'

I watch Marthe's hands as she places one prawn after the next on Olea's plate, her fingers are shorter and stubbier than mine, and she bites her nails, she always has. Twisting the head off, squeezing the back, pulling off the tail, peeling away the shell. I take a few prawns from my plate and lay them on Olea's. Marthe looks up at me.

'What are you doing?' she asks.

'I just thought Olea might like them,' I say. 'It just saves her waiting while the rest of us are eating.'

'Are you really going to make a thing about how fast I peel prawns?' Marthe asks.

I hold my slice of bread with both hands and take a large bite. The prawns are good, they are, firm as I sink my teeth into them. Marthe snorts with laughter for a moment, looking at Mum and then at Kristoffer.

'I gave Olea two prawns,' I say, putting my bread back down, smiling. 'Is that really so bad?'

'Can we not,' Kristoffer says, waving a hand, Olea buries her face in the crook of his arm, just like I did last night, I think to myself.

'Yes,' I say. 'I think Marthe must be a bit hormonal.'

Stein chuckles, Mum shoots an irritated glance in his direction.

'I don't have to listen to this,' Marthe says, shaking her head and pursing her lips, she pushes her chair back with a clatter and stands up.

'Marthe,' Mum says, reaching out for her. 'Don't go.'

Marthe pushes her arm away, slamming the door behind her. Mum looks over at me.

'*Hello!*' I say, feel myself breathing fast, a wave of sudden and glorious fury rising up in me, my hands and feet warm once again. 'It was two prawns, come on. I should be allowed the right to exist here, pregnant or not.'

'It's not about who's pregnant or not,' Mum says.

Stein helps himself to another fistful of prawns, he's finished his first open sandwich already. Kristoffer stares at me, I stare back and he shakes his head.

'Do you want any more prawns, Olea?' he asks, tousling her hair.

'I don't want prawns,' Olea whispers to him, still not looking up. They lie there untouched on her plate, Kristoffer asks if she'd rather have liver pâté on her bread and she nods. She sits with Stein and Mum and me and gazes at the tabletop, none of us are her family, I think to myself, I want to cry when I see the way she hangs her head, she doesn't belong here.

'Don't worry about it, Olea,' Mum says, placing a hand on her neck. 'Grown-ups argue sometimes, then they make up again.'

She looks across the table at me.

'Could you go out and speak to Marthe?' she asks. 'Then we can all just try to have a nice time together.'

'It was *two prawns*,' I say. 'She was the one who lost her rag.'

Marthe is in the hammock, she hasn't removed her shoes, she pushes off with her legs and it swings back and forth. She rests one hand on her belly. As I approach her, she shuffles into an upright position and rubs her face. She's been crying.

'What's going on?' I ask, adopting a friendly tone.

'What's going on?' Marthe repeats. 'You're picking on me, that's what.'

'Doesn't seem like that's the only thing bothering you,' I say.

She inhales with a sob.

'Things are just hard,' she says. 'Between Kristoffer and me.'

I climb into the other end of the hammock, pulling my legs up inside. There isn't really room for two, but when we bend our legs, we just about fit. The hammock wobbles, we have to hold the sides tight until we find a rhythm, rocking back and forth. It was how we always used to sit. The swaying causes my chest to tighten again. It's just the same trees, the pines and cherry trees, the same hammock, this garden, there's something hopeless about the way it never changes, the fact that I'm here, growing older by the day.

'He's completely uninterested,' Marthe says. 'He just goes around with Olea, he hardly even looks at me.'

'Oh,' I say.

'Things have to get better,' Marthe says. 'When the baby comes. I don't get it, don't know if he's depressed or what.'

'I probably shouldn't say this,' I say.

'Say what?' Marthe replies.

We rock back and forth, slowly, slowly, the branches creak. Sitting like this, I used to swing us so fast that Marthe would scream at the top of her lungs, sometimes she'd try to get out mid-swing and would fall on her face. I feel the words on the tip of my tongue, eager to escape, they taste sweet and dark. She ought to know. She can't go around kidding herself about things. These are the kinds of things sisters ought to tell one another, I think to myself, the kinds of things you're obliged to say. You're obliged to say these kinds of things even when it's uncomfortable to do so, I think to myself, feeling myself straighten up where I'm sitting.

'It's the kind of thing you should know,' I say. 'When we were up drinking last night, he told me he didn't want more children.'

'What do you mean?' Marthe asks.

'He's dreading it,' I say. 'Having Olea was the reason things went downhill with his ex. He hates the fact you're pregnant.'

'Stop it,' Marthe says, shifting around in the hammock. 'He couldn't have been happier when we found out.'

'Look,' I say to her. 'I know you're angry at me. But I think I'd want to know about it if my husband was feeling that way about things.'

'So how exactly do you think he's feeling, hmm?' Marthe asks.

'*I* don't think anything,' I tell her. 'He told me about some dinner before the summer with some couple you know, Kristian and Ann, where you'd said no when they'd offered you wine, and people had started to speculate, and he told me that all he could think was that he hoped you'd miscarry.'

Marthe blinks hard, looks down at her hands.

'I'm sure it was Kristian and Ann,' I say.

'Yes,' she mumbles. 'We went to dinner with them.'

'I feel like you deserve better,' I say, scratching my leg. I've been bitten by a mosquito, a huge, swollen bulge, I scratch it as hard as I can.

'Why did he tell you that?' Marthe asks.

Her face has frozen in some sort of grimace, as if she were in physical pain.

'I guess he needed someone to talk to,' I say. 'We'd had a lot to drink. It was pretty uncomfortable, really, I was just like *hey there, you can't be telling me this.*'

I look up in the direction of the cabin, Kristoffer is sitting in the doorway looking down at us. Why did they paint it white, couldn't it have been left yellow?

'It was pretty uncomfortable,' I say again.

Marthe swings her legs around and out of the hammock, her eyes are streaming. She stamps across the grass and walks straight past Kristoffer, he reaches out to grab her wrist and she lashes out in his direction as she passes him by. He glances over at me before following her inside. I lie back, kicking off from the ground beneath me and picking up speed, something quivers within me, something in the region of my diaphragm burns, a kind of queasy feeling, and I lie there and gaze upwards as I swing from side to side. The hammock smells of mildew, it must be almost as old as I am, it reminds me of biscuits and juice and Donald Duck comic books, with their tales of Scamp and Li'l Bad Wolf and Big Bad Wolf, tall blades of grass that you could cut yourself on. I hear loud voices coming from the cabin, the door leading out into the garden is open and I can hear every word they're saying, then after a while I hear fast-paced footsteps making their way down the gravel path and a car starting up, I lie still and listen to everything, feel wide open, my own pulse drumming in my ears.

An hour later, Marthe still hasn't returned. I sit on the sofa and watch kids' TV with Olea, she's quiet and fidgety.

'I don't like her out driving like this, not when she's so worked up,' Mum says again, looking up. 'She could veer right off the road.'

She and Stein set a jigsaw puzzle out on the kitchen table, it's one they brought with them, some Disneyesque castle in Germany. They like doing jigsaws together, she's told us. Stein says it's good for the nerves, so when Marthe doesn't pick up the phone and Mum can't calm herself down, he fetches the box containing all one thousand pieces.

'It'll be OK,' I repeat, then get up. 'We have to stop imagining the worst. Does anyone want a cup of tea?'

'Please,' Mum says, smiling, grateful, I pat her shoulder and she strokes the back of my hand, holds on to it. Stein wants a cup of tea too. We've had some of the birthday cake we picked up at the bakery in town along the coast, it was decorated with marzipan and roses, I tidy away the plates and scrape the leftover pieces of marzipan into the bin.

'Are you going to ask Kristoffer too?' Mum asks.

We look out the window. Kristoffer is sitting on the decking with his back to us, still with his phone to his ear, then he puts it back down and appears to be texting.

'He's still trying to get through to Marthe,' I say. 'But it doesn't look like she's picking up.'

'It must have been awful for you,' Mum whispers so that Olea can't hear her.

'It was,' I whisper back, pouring water into the teapot. 'But worse for Marthe, obviously.'

'Coming out with something like that,' Mum says. 'No, poor Marthe. Gosh.'

'We just have to make the best of it, even if he did show himself up,' I say. 'Look after Olea, you know.'

Stein peers at us over his spectacles, finds a piece of his puzzle and pops it into place. I don't want to look at him. My armpits are sweating. He doesn't know anything, I think to myself, he doesn't know anything about Marthe or me or Mum, he doesn't belong here either, I feel my exasperation growing, why should he be here, why can't he just leave, too?

I pass Mum and Stein their cups of tea, then pour some cereal into a bowl for Olea and add milk, sit down beside her on the sofa. The kids' TV programmes come to an end and an advert comes on for a summer talk show airing later today, the presenter is shouting with a big smile on her face, almost too wide, as if she had more teeth than everyone else. She is standing beside a chef who is smiling straight at the camera while squinting, he's wearing a chef's hat and white apron. They focus the camera on a pan containing a pink shellfish soup. I can see Oslo fjord and Aker Brygge in the background, try to work out where the studio is located, perhaps it's up by Akershus Fortress.

'Take a look at this,' the presenter says, gazing down at the pan.

'Yes,' the chef says, 'not long to go now.'

'Shall we start getting ready for bed, Olea?' I ask.

She shakes her head without taking her eyes from the screen. I wrap a hand around one of her feet, rubbing it. Her foot is bare and a little cold, bare and round and as soft as any cuddly toy where it rests in my hand. I run my fingers along the sole of her foot until she giggles and pulls away.

'Was it horrible seeing Marthe and Dad argue?' I ask her.

'A bit,' she whispers, sucking on her lower lip.

'Maybe you and I could take a little trip out in the boat before bedtime?' I suggest. 'Go fishing?'

'With a fishing rod?' Olea asks as she looks up at me, more alert now.

'With a handline,' I reply. 'You can have your own line. We'll see if we can catch anything.'

'Can we take the big boat out?' Olea asks.

'Sure,' I tell her.

'What a nice idea,' Mum says, winking at Olea from across her puzzle and smiling at us both. Something about all this feels so right, I sense it, I'm the grown-up now, I'm good at this. My tone is calm and kind, it feels familiar, like how things ought to be. I find Olea's life jacket hanging from the peg in the hallway along with a pair of trainers and a coat, feel almost proud to see her standing there ready to go with her life jacket on, looking excited. See, Marthe, I can do this, I'm the one who's supposed to be doing this.

We have to pass Kristoffer on our way down to the jetty. He's sitting on the decking having a cigarette, an empty coffee cup beside him, gripping the phone hard in one hand, I can see that he's been crying. As we walk past him with our fishing gear and bucket, he looks up.

'It's time for her to go to bed,' he says.

'I thought it might be nice for us to take a little trip out in the boat before bedtime,' I tell him. 'Olea thought so, too.'

'I'm going to have my own handline,' Olea says, her voice timid, I'm not even sure she knows what a handline is.

'That's not for you to decide,' Kristoffer says to me, his jaw clenched.

Olea freezes beside me, he must look scary to her in this moment, red-faced, an unfamiliar expression on his face.

'We don't *have* to go fishing,' she mumbles quietly, tugging at my hand.

'Of course we do, let's go,' I say.

The sea is greyish as I drive us out across the fjord, the evening light dwindling. There aren't as many boats out as usual, and it feels a little less steady today, the boat feels more cumbersome to manoeuvre. Olea is lying on her stomach on the deck with one arm stretched out over the side of the boat, she looks back every so often and smiles at me as the waves slosh upwards and wet her arm. I remember what it felt like to lie like that, one ear against the side of the boat, my hand covering the other ear as I listened to the lapping of the waves and the dull thuds that seemed to come from within the boat, as if it harboured a secret that it never told a soul.

'I'm allowed to lie here, aren't I?' she says.

'Of course you are,' I tell her. 'As long as you hold on tight to the line.'

'Daddy says I'm not allowed,' she says.

'You're allowed when you're with me,' I reply.

She shuffles forward, her upper body leaning over the edge. My head feels constrained, as if I'm observing the world through some kind of filter. I hear my doctor over and over again, snatches of our conversation, *enjoying the summer? I'm sorry*. The waves are more powerful than they were yesterday, I stare down at the water as I guide the boat over the swells, and for a moment I catch a glimpse of the catastrophe films I've seen, a huge wave rolling in our direction and flipping the boat over. We don't need to be out here fishing for long, I think to myself, inwardly I hope we don't actually catch anything, I don't know if I've got it in me to kill something while Olea watches. Marthe's probably never taken Olea out in the boat alone, she's only just learnt to take it out herself. I wonder where she's gone, if she's sitting crying somewhere, I feel vaguely sick at the thought. It was easy to say all that I did about Kristoffer, it shouldn't have been that easy.

A cabin cruiser passes us by, it keeps to the right but is moving fast and the waves pick up. We dip up and down, I pull the steering wheel hard to one side and open my mouth to tell Olea to hold on tight, but I'm too late. Olea has been lying with her upper body hanging over the edge of the boat and her legs straight out behind her. She flips over the side as the boat is thrown up into the air and tumbles into the water, I call out, can't hear the sound of my own shout. I see her head in the water, her arms, I can't stop the boat, all of a sudden I can't remember what you're supposed to do in a situation like this, is there a button to push, some kind of brake somewhere, what are you supposed to do, should I jump out to swim to her, I fumble and try reversing the boat, but I've forgotten how to do that too, my hands are shaking, my mind turns white and vacant and cold, I can hear only the drone of the engine as the boat pushes me onwards, it's going too fast, moving further and further away from her. Eventually I manage to swing it around in a curve and drive back. I can't see her at first, the fjord is endlessly vast and every wave looks the same, the same colour, the same shape, I can't see her, the sobs chafe at the inside of my ribcage, this isn't happening, it's not happening, then I see her head and her arms as she struggles in the water, not as far away as I'd previously thought. I put the engine into neutral and lie on my stomach, I grab the collar of her life vest and she screams and flails so strongly that I lose my grip, she grabs my arm with both hands and clings on tight. She's surprisingly heavy as I haul her over the side of the boat. Her clothes are drenched, she's lost a shoe and her knee is bleeding, she must have scraped it on something. I kneel down beside her, her mouth is twisted open in a silent scream, then the sound comes. She howls a loud and deep and terrible howl, clings to me as I hug her tight.

'Shall we do a little fishing and see if that makes you feel any better?' I ask her, I'm hot with shame.

'I want to go home,' Olea cries.

'OK,' I say. 'Let's go back.'

I remain faintly hopeful that she might have calmed down a bit by the time we get back, that we might be able to make out that it was a funny little turn of events, look at us, what are we like, Olea, but as we approach the jetty, it's as if the volume is turned up all over again. She leaps back on land before I manage to stop her, her shoe gurgling, her clothes schlipp-schlapping, she runs towards the cabin wailing. I moor up, moving quickly and clumsily. By the time I make it up to the garden, she's sitting on Kristoffer's lap as he rocks her.

'We had a little accident,' I say.

Olea is shivering and shivering.

'She was wearing her life vest,' I say, I can hear how bad it all sounds, but she was wearing her life vest.

Mum and Stein have both come out onto the decking now, and Mum asks what happened, Olea's soaking-wet clothing and hair, her missing shoe, her grazed knee. Olea regales them with what happened in one long, loud stream, her story interrupted only by her sobbing, she's making more of it than she needs to, I think to myself, she shouts that she was lying down at the front of the boat, Aunt Ida said she was allowed, and then she fell overboard and Aunt Ida kept going. I want to tell her to be quiet, don't say anything else, be quiet, but I can't, I have to stand there and listen to her, her weeping and whining.

'I didn't keep going, Olea,' I say, I'm standing with my arms by my sides, I'm on the verge of tears, I picture her there in the water, the feeling I had when I couldn't see her, the blood on her knee.

'You *kept going*?' Kristoffer says.

'Not on purpose,' I say. 'I couldn't stop the boat.'

'You need to be careful when you've got children on board, Ida,' Mum says. 'You're really not that familiar with driving the boat.'

'I'm well aware of that,' I shout, a lump in my throat.

'She could have drowned,' Kristoffer says. 'What exactly were you doing, anyway, were you sitting there texting or something?'

'She was wearing her life vest,' I repeat.

'You can drown even when wearing a life vest, you know,' Stein says, polishing his glasses. 'They give people a false sense of security.'

'Weren't you drinking at lunchtime?' Mum asks.

'That was ages ago,' I say. 'Jesus.'

'And I lost my shoe,' Olea says. 'My new shoe.'

'You're a good girl,' Mum says, I think she's talking to me at first, but it's Olea she's looking at as she strokes her wet hair. We stand around Kristoffer and Olea in a semi-circle, Mum, Stein and me, and the others are all looking at me, they're looking at me, all four of them, as if they're

132

waiting for me to say something, but I say nothing, I don't know what to say. I look up to try to stop myself from crying, see the white cabin wall, the roof tiles and eaves, we've had a wasps' nest there a few times over the years. Kristoffer stands up with Olea in his arms, he says it's time to get her out of her wet clothes, her teeth are chattering. He promises her sweets and she asks him if she needs to clean her teeth and he tells her that she can skip it tonight.

'You need to apologise properly, Ida,' Mum says.

'I didn't do it on purpose,' I say.

Stein raises his eyebrows at me and smiles weakly, I look away.

A little later on, I peek into the bedroom as Kristoffer is putting Olea to bed. I hear them chatting quietly in the half-darkness. Kristoffer gets up out of the bed when he sees me, we stand in the doorway whispering.

'I don't think you should be here right now,' he says.

'I just want to talk to Olea,' I tell him.

'She doesn't want to talk to you,' he says. 'So just stop.'

'I'm sure she won't mind if I have a quick word with her,' I say.

'Do you know what?' Kristoffer says, stepping out into the hallway where I'm standing and closing the door behind him. 'Olea and I are the ones who are family here. You're not a part of that. I'm not going to lay into Marthe the way you do, and you need to understand when it's time to keep your fucking distance. OK?'

'You don't want that baby,' I say, it comes out like a hiss.

He says nothing, simply shakes his head and returns to Olea. I can see her in the bed, she locks eyes with me and turns to face the wall. Kristoffer sits on the edge of her bed and looks at me until I give up and close the door.

I PULL MY CLOTHES out of the wardrobe in the tiny room, fold what's on the chair, gather up the books and magazines and put everything inside my bag. It's getting dark outside. The garden is so nice at night, the bushes look like dark animals or shadowy figures, a few of Olea's toys lie abandoned on the grass. The hammock sways in the wind, as if someone had just been lying inside and hopped out. Out on the fjord, lanterns pass each other by, green, red. I watch the lights as I rest a hand on my lower abdomen, try to get a sense of whether anything is still working in there, whether anything there might be able to support life, or if it's simply silent and flat and dead. All I feel is skin, warm beneath my hand. I'll ask one of the others to drive me to the bus stop tomorrow, it'll have to be Mum or perhaps even Stein, I'll go back to my flat and be alone, feel that lonesomeness enfold me, I can watch TV and sleep in every day, right up until I'm due back at work, I don't need to speak to any of them, all will be silent.

Mum sticks her head in the door and asks what I'm doing. She doesn't knock, either.

'Packing,' I tell her. 'I'm going tomorrow.'

'You're going?' she says. 'Why?'

'We're heading back soon anyway,' I say. 'I just fancy a bit of time to myself in the city.'

She stands there with her arms crossed, peering at me over her reading glasses, she looks just like Marthe standing there like that, and I feel my temper flaring up at the fact that she has to stand there like that, to look the way she does, lingering there and shifting her weight from her left foot to her right, all when she doesn't need to be here, it's enough to tip a person over the edge.

'Did you want something?' I ask.

'Is something wrong?' she asks, that fumbling she does, why does she have to do everything so slowly, I feel breathless with impatience.

'I'm fine,' I reply, turning a jumper inside out before folding it.

'You're acting so strangely,' Mum says.

'I'm not,' I retort, as if I'm thirteen years old, but I never said anything like that when I was thirteen, not as far as I can remember anyway, Marthe would slam doors and tear strips off Mum during puberty, creating drama whenever she wasn't allowed something she wanted, and all the while I acted the grown-up, looking at Mum and shaking my head at how impossible Marthe was being. I never did more than I was allowed to, I consoled Mum when Marthe was unwell or being unreasonable, I was there by her side; I feel the injustice, rampant and raging, there's no one to console me, poor old me, not a single soul to console me,

I can't carry on like this, lamenting things that happened a lifetime ago.

Mum crosses her arms and leans against the doorframe.

'Can't we at least try to have a nice time together for these last few days?' she says. 'Are you willing to try?'

I can't face her irritation. I've never been able to. I look at the clothes I've placed in my bag, my arms awkward and heavy by my sides.

'Things will work themselves out once Marthe gets back,' Mum says. 'Then we'll have a barbecue tomorrow, what do you say?'

I nod, feel myself clenching my fists, my eyes welling up.

'OK,' I say.

'Lovely,' Mum says, her tone vaguely impatient, she pats my shoulder before leaving the room.

I LIE CURLED UP under a blanket in the hammock and
gaze upwards; brightness lingers in the twilight, a summer
sky. My stomach is hollow, I've not eaten enough, feel dizzy.
I'm not just sad, the hammock rocks slowly from side to
side, I'm not just sad. My hands and feet are warmer now,
my pulse is moving through my body with intense force.
What if nothing turns out the way I'd expected. What if
there's something else, something different from everything
I've imagined. Something a little more ordinary. Something
a little happier.

Then I hear the car, half get up, the thud of the car
door and Marthe's footsteps on the gravel, then the cabin
door opening and slamming closed again. I can hear that
it's her, there's something about the rhythm. It's the sort
of thing that sisters know, I think to myself, how to hurt
one another, what one another's footsteps sound like,
moving through the house at night, on a gravel path by
the cabin.

———

I can smell cigarette smoke from the decking, someone is sitting there, it's Stein. I bring my blanket, sit down with him and take a cigarette from the packet lying on the table, Kristoffer's packet. It must be a few years since I last smoked. I inhale, feel the numbing spread of the nicotine across my chest, the way it pulses through my arms and hands. The new garden chairs are comfortable, I sink back, feel like I'm lying in bed.

'Ida, Ida, Ida,' Stein says.

'Stein, Stein, Stein,' I reply.

'That's me,' Stein says, chuckling.

'Are Marthe and Kristoffer talking?' I ask.

'Yes,' Stein says. 'I thought it might be a good idea to make myself scarce.'

We sit there in silence, I flinch as a mosquito whistles past my ear, bat it away.

'I thought the smoke might help keep the mosquitoes at bay,' Stein says.

'Why don't you have any children?' I ask him.

'Why don't I have any children?' he repeats, scratching the space between his eyes. 'It just never happened. The woman I was married to, she wasn't able to. It might have been possible these days, what with all the technological advances and that sort of thing. But.'

The mosquito has landed on my arm. I raise my hand as I watch it, it readies its tiny proboscis and plunges it into my skin, I flick it away.

'Don't you have any regrets about that?' I ask.

'Watching you all on this holiday, you mean?' Stein asks and guffaws, and I laugh to myself too.

'There are regrets and then there are *regrets*,' he says eventually. 'I don't know what there is to regret, in this case. From time to time I think to myself that it might have been nice. It could have been really nice. But it's no worse than occasionally missing a long-dead grandmother, for instance.'

I say nothing. My skin itches where the mosquito landed.

'It can be just fine, this life, Ida,' he says, looking at me. 'I think it's a good life. There are lots of different ways to live.'

A good life, I think to myself. For a moment I imagine myself turning into Stein when I'm older, a middle-aged, childless effeminate man with clip-on sunglasses that fit over my normal frames and a fedora hat that I insist on wearing on the boat even though everyone rolls their eyes at me.

Marthe steps out onto the decking. She's in her stockinged feet and looks exhausted.

'Here's Marthe come to join us,' Stein says.

'Yep,' Marthe says.

She sits on the ground beside my legs.

'Here, take a seat,' Stein says, standing up. 'Women and children, and all that. I'll see how things are going inside.'

Marthe had gone into town, she had booked a room in the hotel by the fjord and had planned on staying there until morning. But there was a noisy pub a few floors below, with people shouting at the tops of their voices all night and loud music streaming from the beer garden, she couldn't sleep, she sat in the hotel bed and watched TV and had to turn the sound up to drown out the music from downstairs, they'd started playing old summer hits, probably the same song I'd heard from the boat the other night, and in the end all she could think about was her own bed.

'Anyway, I had to talk to Kristoffer sooner or later,' she says, attempting a smile and breaking down halfway.

'Has he gone to bed?' I ask.

'Yes,' she says, waving her hands. 'Fuck. Ugh, I don't want to cry anymore.'

She snivels, breathing with her mouth open. I get up and find a blanket for her, the evening air is cold and damp.

'The worst part of it is the fact he never said anything,' she says. 'He just pretended to be happy about the whole thing. He could have said.'

'But nothing might have come of it all,' I say. 'You got what you wanted.'

'Yes,' she says. 'Yes. But I didn't think I'd be sitting here, pregnant with the child of a man who was dead set against the idea,' she says, looking down at her stomach, as if it's suddenly unfamiliar to her.

I take another cigarette from Kristoffer's packet, picture what I imagine Marthe is picturing, Kristoffer laden with the weight of his guilty conscience, a man with no interest in attending antenatal classes, a man bottling up his annoyance with Marthe after the birth, growing more and more exhausted every time the baby wails, Marthe getting up all night long, more often than she can really manage because she's afraid that Kristoffer will be annoyed if he has to do it, and one day he says it anyway, *Marthe, I can't do this anymore.*

'You can buy me out,' I say. 'I've thought about it. It's fine.'

'Really?' Marthe says, trying to look indifferent, but she's pleased, it's not hard to see it. 'That's great.'

I nod. She's stopped crying, the blanket is pulled up to her chin and her legs are curled up on the chair.

Then I tell her about Sweden, I tell her about the phone call I received yesterday and what the doctor told me.

'Ohh,' Marthe says. 'Does that mean it's all over?'

'Don't know,' I reply. 'I think it makes things difficult, at the very least.'

Marthe nods. A branch creaks somewhere in the garden.

'It's just so stupid,' I say, and feel myself starting to cry. 'It's not as if I *have* to have children, you know? Or, I don't know. Maybe. It's just so final, in a way. I hadn't ever imagined it would suddenly be too late. It's stupid.'

'It's not stupid,' Marthe says.

'No,' I reply.

We fall silent.

'You might be onto something after all,' Marthe says, laughing quietly. 'I don't think I'm cut out for it. I'm no good with Olea. I get the feeling Kristoffer thinks that too.'

It almost tears me apart, the pain in her smile, her sisterly gaze. I shake my head. Something opens up within me, just as it had during dinner, I've gone about everything the wrong way. There's a void within me and it's growing, taking over, it is as if I'm staring into something vast and black, something staring back at me.

'What's wrong?' Marthe asks.

Sorry sorry sorry sorry. For doing the things I do. For being the way I am. For everything I can't do and can't face. I feel the words pushing from within, they want out, *it wasn't Kristoffer's fault*, but I don't know if that's true, either. Marthe gets up and hugs me, it feels awkward and too tight as I try to prise myself free from her grasp.

'What's wrong?' she asks again, sounding sympathetic.

Of course she's being kind now, now that I've given her the cabin, now that I've given her the path down to the bathing spot and the old playhouse and the hammock between the pine trees, it hurts already. I take a few deep breaths in through my nose, pull myself together.

'It's nothing,' I say.

I DIDN'T SLEEP too well, didn't drift off until it started to grow light. My body aches, my chest and arms, a rolling sensation fills my head, I get up slowly and draw the curtains. It's so nice here, so pretty with the morning sunlight and the water, the screeching of gulls, everything is clear and bright. I hear the others, voices and sounds elsewhere in the house.

'Hi,' Marthe says as I step into the kitchen. She and Kristoffer and Olea are sitting at the kitchen table. Kristoffer looks away.

'Hi,' I say.

I pour myself a cup of coffee, I don't know where to sit at first, end up taking a seat beside Marthe. The others are having boiled eggs, there are none for me, my head is abuzz with the thought that I ought to make some sort of joke about it, but I don't know who I'd tell it to, Marthe, maybe.

'It feels a bit like the day after the night before in that film, *Festen*,' I say, and when there's no response, I add: 'You know that scene the next morning, when the paedo Dad has been exposed and tries to find a place at the table.'

Nobody laughs.

'What's a paedo?' Olea asks.

'Nothing,' Marthe replies.

Kristoffer and Marthe are sitting side by side, both looking exhausted, Marthe is puffy-eyed. Kristoffer sneaks the occasional concerned glance in her direction.

'We're leaving today,' Marthe says. 'We've got… things to work out.'

I look at Olea, her ponytail and half-open mouth as she chews, her slim shoulders in her purple vest, her gaze lazily fixed on an obscure point in thin air. Everything she's thinking, everything she says, everything she can do, everything she's going to become, everything that won't ever be mine, the sorrow swells within me all over again, I close my eyes and feel myself losing my footing, overcome by the wave. Time has passed me by, silently, without me ever realising it, it's sneaked through the room as I've slept. Somewhere down there is a hard sense of relief, too: there's no longer anything to worry about.

I look at Marthe, buttering another slice of bread, Kristoffer drinking his coffee and fiddling with his phone, Olea idly wiggling a loose tooth, soon they'll be four, at least as things stand, it would take so little for things to crack. A single sentence, one utterance, anything that might suggest that they don't really know each other after all, and they'd go their separate ways again.

Kristoffer gazes at the contents of his mug, lips pursed. I won't ask for his forgiveness. I look at the plates with their floral embellishments and the milk glasses, I've given them all of this, it's enough; a burning regret sears through me when I think about the fact that it's Marthe who's going to own this place, I shouldn't have done it, shouldn't have done it.

'I'm sorry I wasn't as careful as I could have been on our trip out, Olea,' I say, looking at her. 'I didn't keep going without you on purpose, I just couldn't stop the boat.'

Olea nods, she looks away and continues to fiddle with her loose tooth.

'Can I see your tooth?' I ask.

She shakes her head. Marthe looks at me, I feel my cheeks burning.

WE WAVE THEM OFF. Mum and Stein and I stand side by side and watch their car as they drive away, Olea waves out of the back window as energetically as she can, in the end she has to switch hands; as they turn the corner I see Marthe's arm appear out of her window, a feeble wave of her hand before the car disappears out of sight.

'And that was that,' Mum says, shaking her hands. 'Gosh, it always feels so quiet when people leave.'

'A little coffee, maybe?' Stein suggests, patting her shoulder.

I lie down on the sofa and browse the cabin's guest book, the others wrote in it before leaving. Olea has drawn herself holding two large fish with a wide, slightly wonky stroke of a smile, and beneath it Marthe has written half a page. I recognise her handwriting from our teenage years, very proper and slightly childish, I rarely ever see it these days. 'Thanks for a lovely few days,' she's written, then a bit about the weather, up-and-down for the first few days with a fair bit of rain, but better after that. There have been trips to the town along the coast for ice cream and a few hikes to Heia, too, lots of ticks this year, they all had to check themselves thoroughly, Olea caught her first ever fish and Marthe took the big boat out, it's never too late to learn! 'We celebrated Mum's 65th birthday with prawns and a delicious cake, and Ida joined us for a few days, too,' she writes towards the end. 'We've had a lovely holiday, and now it's back to normality for us.'

I'd expected to read something about there being four of them next time, that would have been typical of Marthe, but she's written nothing. I flick back through previous entries, always the same reports, mostly from Marthe and Mum, with the odd virtually illegible sentence from Stein underneath, as well as a few entries written by Mum and Stein's friends who have come to stay and who are brimming with praise. It's all thunder and sunshine and fishing and ticks and staining the decking and sorting out the boat and what's been on the menu, Mum writes over and over again about beautiful cod, mackerel straight from the fjord, fresh prawns, Stein's red wine casserole. I've only written in it twice. Bathing, hammock, fishing, 'big thanks from me!', both entries are from the end of August, otherwise my name only ever appears as an additional signature on something Mum's written. I should have come here more often, or I should have come in a different way, nobody would know I'd ever been here at all. I clap the book together, slip it back on its shelf, step out onto the decking outside, the planks of wood beneath my feet have been warmed by the sun. Mum and Stein are each sitting in their own garden chair, Stein is working on a crossword, Mum is reading a book. She's wearing sunglasses and bats away a wasp that buzzes around her, the wasp returns and she hits out at it again. I stand there and watch them, there's a chair free, a magazine is lying on the table, but I can't bring myself to pick it up and sit with them.

Mum removes her sunglasses and looks at me.

'What's wrong?' she asks.

'I want you both to go,' I say.

'WILL YOU BE OK on your own?' Mum asks.

'I'll be fine,' I reply.

Stein carries their bags out to the car. I'm sure that he was the one who persuaded her to leave two days earlier than planned, Mum sulked as she packed up yesterday evening. Stein gives me a brief pat on the shoulder before climbing inside the car and closing the door behind him, I hear him turn the radio on.

'Well, I can't say I know exactly what you're up to, I must admit,' Mum says, laughing angrily. 'All this, out of the blue.'

'Yes,' I say.

She's annoyed with me, but it doesn't matter, I register her irritation and feel nothing, just a sense of fatigue in every last limb.

'What are you going to do now?' she asks.

'I'll see,' I say.

'Well, I'm sure you will,' Mum says. 'Ida and Marthe, you two always do as you like. What was it you said in that speech you gave?'

'Fail better?' I reply.

'No, your speech yesterday,' Mum says. 'Life begins at forty, wasn't that it?'

'You were the one who said that,' I say.

We give each other something approaching a hug, it feels awkward. I stand on the gravel pathway and wave at the car until it disappears around the corner, then I go back inside, closing the door behind me. It's silent here now, every room empty, the sun shines in through the windows, falling on the floorboards and rag rug, revealing a layer of dust on the shelf with its row of old shells and framed marine map. Time ticks onwards throughout the cabin and its garden and me, no one summer easily distinguishable from another, which year was it that was so hot, which summer was it that we caught all those mackerel, some will be gone soon, others will arrive.

I move my things out of the tiny bedroom and into the large one. Then I go out onto the decking and look out at the fjord. It's only me here. I stand there in silence and feel the sun on my face.

TOPICS FOR DISCUSSION

1. Ida and Marthe sometimes seem to be trapped in the dynamic that they had as young girls. Do you think that we outgrow our childhood sibling relationships?

2. Which of the book's characters did you relate to the most?

3. Did this novel change your opinions on what it means to be an adult? Did you find that it called any of your assumptions about adulthood into question?

4. Ida has plenty of opinions on how Marthe and Kristoffer are raising Olea – opinions, however, that she rarely voices. Why do you think that this is?

5. *Grown Ups* is written exclusively from Ida's point of view – did being so fully immersed in Ida's perspective make you more sympathetic to her? Were there any moments where you actively disagreed with her?

6. How do the parenting styles of Mum and Stein compare to Marthe and Kristoffer?

7. How did you view Ida's relationship with Olea?

8. What do Ida's feelings about the family cabin, and about how she is becoming side-lined in the ownership of the cabin, say about her status as a 'grown up' within her family?

AVAILABLE AND COMING SOON
FROM PUSHKIN PRESS

Pushkin Press was founded in 1997, and publishes novels, essays, memoirs, children's books—everything from timeless classics to the urgent and contemporary.

Our books represent exciting, high-quality writing from around the world: we publish some of the twentieth century's most widely acclaimed, brilliant authors such as Stefan Zweig, Yasushi Inoue, Teffi, Antal Szerb, Gerard Reve and Elsa Morante, as well as compelling and award-winning contemporary writers, including Dorthe Nors, Edith Pearlman, Perumal Murugan, Ayelet Gundar-Goshen and Chigozie Obioma.

Pushkin Press publishes the world's best stories, to be read and read again. To discover more, visit www.pushkinpress.com.

MS ICE SANDWICH
MIEKO KAWAKAMI

LEARNING TO TALK TO PLANTS
MARTA ORRIOLS

MY BROTHER
KARIN SMIRNOFF

WILL
JEROEN OLYSLAEGERS

THE COLLECTED STORIES OF STEFAN ZWEIG
STEFAN ZWEIG

THE EVENINGS
GERARD REVE